In a Nut's Hell

LITERARY DOODLES

C
O
M
E
D
Y
!

i
E
R
I
T
A
S

JIM WOOD

Book Inside

Deluxe Edition With Profanity!

BITE-SIZED STORIES!

outskirts
press

PRAISE FOR "IN A NUT'S HELL"

"Serious silliness..."
Jim Woodkin, *The Daily Weekly*

"Silly seriousness..."
James Woodlawn, *Sacramento Beaver*

"Not to be taken lightly..."
Jim Woodford, *Uppity-Type Gazette*

"Not to be taken seriously..."
James Woodblock, *American Journal of Anal Disorders*

"At long last, Wood provides a much-needed voice for...
well, for Wood."
J. Wellington Woodford, *Illiterate's Digest*

"...groundbreaking, if published in 1653..."
J.J. Woodpecky, *Journal of Whatevs and Stuff*

"This book adds nothing, because it is not a calculator."
Renaldo "The Equation" Mathface, *Mathematics Monthly*

"...offbeat, yet literary; entertaining; a few typos..."
Gary Wood

"Shut up, Jimmy."
The Rest of Jim Wood's family

"This is a book made of paper with words enabled by ink."
Literal

A NOTE OF THANKS

I'd like to thank The Following People, which is a name I've given to the group of people who have ever followed me, either by design (because they are interested in and entertained by my artistic pursuits, are stalking me, etc) or inadvertently (those behind me on line at the supermarket checkout, those following me up subway stairs, etc). I could have written this book without them, and I did, so thank you from the upper third of my heart. I'd also like to thank myself, without whom I couldn't.

WARNINGS!

This book is not for everyone. If it was, I'd be the best-selling author of all time. Do not read this book if:

1. You are easily or unable to be offended
2. You have a relationship with me in which I am forced to behave somewhat normally
3. You cannot read
4. You really should be doing something else
5. You are squeamish
6. You are Amish
7. You're from Squamish

Thank you for your patience.
The book will begin momentarily.

Excuse me, that's my cell...I have to take this...

Apologies. My Mom, on fire again.

The book is gonna start now.

TABLE OF CONTENTS

A READING FROM THE BOOK YOU'RE READING

"The Lord giveth, the Lord taketh, the Lord bestoweth, and the Lord rewardeth."

"Is this all true, Father Muther?"

"Oh, yeth."

Father Muther had led the holy scientific expedition to explore the possibility that Christ's body actually *was* made of communion wafers, and still no one respected him. Attendance at his church was way down. The good Father had tried everything from LA-Z Boy pews to Cheese Wiz on the communion wafers, but nothing seemed to draw the sinners. How was he to know that some prankster had carved a triple 6 into the back of his head as he daydreamed?

"I turn my back to my congregation, and the next thing I know, they're all gone," he told the Pope, who was signing autographs at White Castle. The Pope, John Paul George Ringo III, one of the pranksters who had carved the sign 'o the beast in the Father's cranium, suppressed a grin and said something in Latin akin to "maybe you just overheard someone else's calling."

Finally, Muther got hip and tapped a fresh keg at every mass. Standing room only.

The good Father had just begun the sermon when suddenly his entire congregation began to stalk, attack, and devour each other.

"HOLD IT! HOLD IT!" shouted the Father, "I meant 'PRAY'!! Let us 'PRAY,' with an 'A,' you idiots!!"

But it was too late. Blood flowed under the pews, collecting in a puddle five feet from the drain. Father Muther got right on the telephone.

"Hello, Holy Cross Construction? Yeah, get over here right away. This drain you installed isn't functioning...No, it's not clogged, it's in the wrong spot or something."

Holy Cross Construction, unable to determine just where the drain should be, made the entire church floor a drain. They didn't question the good Father about the limbless, mutilated churchgoers strewn about the place, being good Christians.

Father Muther shared a hot tub with Sister Bruther that night, still upset over the drain.

"Now they've made the entire floor a drain," he complained, turning on the whirlpool. "I can see a lot of collection money being lost through that drain, you know, dropped by the young and unhealed."

And that was when the idea hit him to make the entire floor a collection plate instead of a drain.

"Your congregation may argue that a collection plate floor *is* a drain," Sister Bruther quipped, surprising Father Muther by speaking for the first time in her life.

"You're healed!" exclaimed the Father, removing her bodycast. He was shocked to see the Ten Commandments tattooed on her left buttock. He was even more shocked to see her left buttock. By removing the Sister's bodycast, he had exposed himself to the sins of the flesh. And he liked it. He threw his collar to the wind and read the Ten Commandments. Closely.

"Last Calling," boomed Him from The Heavens, Inc., giving Muther one last chance to redeem his life's purpose. But it was no use. Father Muther, having had his first orgasm, was already doing cocaine and listening to Frank Zappa. The Lord would have none of this. In his kind and merciful way, he filled the hot tub with piranhas, laying waste to the two who had gone astray.

"It's a dog eat dog food world out there," spaketh the Lord, "but I wouldn't have created it any other way."

WORSER

"I'm in a same sex marriage," quipped Waldorf to no one's amusement, "My wife and I have been having the same sex for 20 years."

"It could always be worse," Nail retorted, opening his 30th beer (an ex-alcoholic, Nail had quit drinking again again, but still opened beers without drinking them as part of his therapy, which he created himself while drunk).

"Y'know, logically, there should be one person on Earth to whom the comforting phrase 'it could always be worse' cannot be uttered," hypothesized Project, just arising from a year-long coma.

"Yes…indeed, yes," mused Waldorf, "…so you're saying that there is one single person on Earth, one poor unfortunate soul, for whom things cannot be any worse?"

"Precisely," confirmed Project, examining the effects of the coma on his face in a mirror that Nail had politely held in front of him for that very purpose. No effects. Good coma.

"And you can't say 'it could always be worse' to this dude,

because it can't be worse for them, right?" asked Nail.

"That's the idea," said Project patiently (Nail was always the last to understand stuff and shit).

"It would be cool to find that miserable so-and-so," chuckled Nail, "just to not say that to him. Or her. Or appropriate non-gender-discriminatory pronoun."

After a 2 millisecond pause and a groundswell of dramatic inspiring music, the three looked at each other in silent determined agreement, set their jaws, and bounded out the door.

———)(()(———

Bladder was surprised to hear the knock at his door, primarily because he had been deaf since birth. On top of that, he had no friends. Thirdly, he didn't have a door. How the hell was this happening?

He looked toward the hole in the front of his house where the door wasn't, and there, where the hole used to be, was a pretty nice (but not great) door from Home Depot, he guessed. He answered it to find three strangers on his porch.

"Hey, how's it goin'?" asked Nail, suppressing a grin.

"Well," said Bladder (deciding not to say "Who are you guys?" or "Can I help you?"), "to be perfectly honest, it's just okay. Somebody put up a door for me for free, but it's just your standard Home Depot deal. I just regained my hearing, but I don't like what I hear so far, especially those cicadas. And, I have no friends."

"It could always be worse!" said Waldorf (the three had used a computer-generated, randomized sequence to assign who would get to deliver this line, and Waldorf's turn was first).

"Hey, I suppose it *could* be worse!" said Bladder cheerily, "I guess I could be 5 payments behind on my 105-foot plasma TV, like Welder next door."

Nail crossed Bladder off his list, and the three made a hasty retreat from Bladder's porch and headed toward Welder's place.

Welder was given the same business, with Project asking "How's it goin'?" and Nail retorting "It could always be worse," and the conversation ended with Welder exclaiming "Of course it could be worse! I could be *7 payments* behind... or, I could have cancer of the conscience like my poor little tall old half-cousin Dirky."

"Cancer!" said Project, mad at himself. "We're wasting our time! We should have started with 'cancer'!"

"Well, it's not like we've done this before," said Waldorf. He looked at his watch. It was getting late, or early, he couldn't tell which. Bottom line: He just was getting the feeling that this was going to take longer than he originally thought.

"Guys," dominated Waldorf, "tight emergency huddle."

The three began to draw closer to each other, and Welder closed his door and went back inside to drink more blood from the elderly homeless man he had recently kidnapped, dragged into his house, and was slowly eating alive. Nail, Waldorf, and Project remained on the porch in their tight emergency huddle.

"Okay guys," said Waldorf, "finding the single person on Earth for whom things cannot get any worse could take as many minutes as there are in years, and I have to go to work in the morning. We need to lay some ground rules here."

"Perhaps we should narrow our search...maybe we should identify the single person for whom things cannot get any worse in America. Or on this block," offered Project.

"That won't work, stupid," said Nail, who himself was stupid. "Because even though they're the most worse on the block, it could always be worse for them compared to that elusive single human that we can't seem to find no matter how hard we try."

"And what if we do find this person," imagined Project, "and it's like, well, he's the worst in the whole world, but, for instance, it could always be worse because, for example, a boulder could be on top of him, or something."

"Well," began Nail, suddenly and uncharacteristically smart as the author chooses the wrong character, "we need to draw the line somewhere. Rule, okay? If we find the worst person, we can't say it could be worse due to something that has no chance of happening, like Project's aforementioned boulder example, or the whole room that he or she is in being filled with vomit or diarrhea. We need to find the single person for whom things cannot get any worse *excluding* things that actually would make things worse but have no chance..."

"...or an infinitesimal chance...," added Welder, sticking his head out a window, his maw dripping with blood.

"...of happening, and yes, thank you, infinitesimal," concluded Nail.

"We could save some time and try Googling 'single person on Earth for whom things cannot get any worse' or whatever," suggested Project.

"Hey guys," said Welder, not exactly fascinated by their conversation but somewhat interested, "I couldn't help but overhear what you were saying because I don't have headphones on...maybe I could save you some time. There's a half-dead homeless person that I recently kidnapped and dragged into my house. I've been slowly eating him alive for days now. Do you think it could get any worse for him?"

The three lit up like three smokers lighting up during an outdoor smoking break.

"Indeed!" exalted Project, "and look!"

Project held up his Personal Pocket Pally Mini-Tiny-Puter, and showed the group the results of the Google search of 'single person on Earth for whom things cannot get any worse' that he had suggested. The single (of course) hit read: homeless dude being slowly eaten alive in Welder's kitchen.

"No wonder that Google stock is so hot," said Welder.

"Google is the totally awesome shit and shit," said Nail.

"How utterly fucking convenient," chirped Waldorf, "and excuse my language, but Jesus Fucking Goddamn Christ All-Goddamn-Fucking-Mighty, can you believe that the single person on Earth for whom things cannot get any worse is inside the second house we went to? Gee Whillikers."

Welder opened the door and the three bounded inside, more excited than a man inventing time travel and planning a trip to the 1950s to perform cunnilingus on Marilyn Monroe (we're all adults here).

They tiptoed into the kitchen, where they saw the elderly homeless man adhered to the countertop with duct tape, his flesh ripped apart, his face bruised beyond recognition, his bones exposed and riddled with Welder's teeth marks. He was barely conscious and moaning softly, resigned and nearly numb to his mind-altering pain. His dim, yellowed eyes stared straight at the ceiling, projecting Hell-on-Earth horror. The three stopped before him, and the man, somebody's baby once, slowly turned his yet-uneaten head toward them.

"Hey, how's it goin'?" asked Waldorf (his turn), grinning wildly along with his comrades in anticipation of not saying you-know-what.

Even the cicadas were silent as Waldorf, Nail, and Project, their faces trembling with excitement, leaned closer to the man in nearly unbridled anticipation of his response. The man's quivering mouth struggled to speak; his unsteady, frothing lips finally parted to offer his reply.

"Can't complain," he croaked, "it's nice to be indoors." He then dropped dead, and Project, sighing in annoyance, got back on Google.

FATHER OF THE NO-METAPHOR LITERARY GENRE

"My pursuit of happiness is to not pursue happiness," spat Angry. "I mean, how can anyone be happy? Look at all the suffering!"

"What suffering? Where?" asked Literal, scanning the room. "Where?"

Literal had been born with a birth defect that rendered him unable to mentally grasp generalizations, similes, expressions, and metaphors. In one particular instance, after attending a Doors concert in 1967, he actually tried to set the night on fire by tossing gasoline-soaked rags up into the air followed quickly by tossed lit matches.

He confronted Jim Morrison after the failed attempt at the premier of an Andy Warhol film, in which Andy's camera rested on the face of a large clock for 36 hours.

"You liar," accused Literal.

Morrison, who had heard this before, delivered his stock reply: "I said 'try' to set the night on fire. I didn't say you'd be successful. What are you going to do next? Swim to the moon?"

"Please accept my apologies," said Literal, embarrassed and humbled. They both sat through the remaining 35 and three-quarter hours of the film in an uncomfortable silence, Literal confused by Morrison's remark about swimming to the moon.

But the hell with Morrison, the night, and the moon. Literal wanted to be an author, and would stop at nothing until he was successful! He spent years trying to figure out how to actually stop at nothing, and failed, but luckily worked on his novel at the same time.

Because of his birth defect, his novel contained no metaphors, no messages, no juxtapositions, no similes, no comparisons...not even adjectives.

Entitled *Man Goes to Work on Tuesday*, it was so devoid of everything that it inadvertently started a No-Metaphor Literary movement. An excerpt follows:

The man got into his car and drove to work. The man parked his car and went into his office.

And another:

The man looked at the clock. It was 4 o'clock. One more hour of work to go. He resumed his task, made a phone call to his supervisor to ask a question about the task, and then incorporated the answer to the question into the task. The man got a drink of water.

The literary world was turned upside down by this new genre, of which Literal was the only author. Try as they might, other would-be authors of the genre simply could not "strip down" their writing to achieve Literal's command of the style.

At the height of his success, Literal was walking down the street against a strong and gusty wind (caused by a block-long fan shop having a sidewalk sale) when he crossed paths with a greasy gentleman in perfectly clean coveralls. The gentleman was carrying papers of some sort, and the strong and gusty wind tore a single sheet from his stack; it flew through the air and affixed itself with great force to Literal's face.

Literal, who had great eyesight, did not remove the paper stuck to his face by the strong and gusty wind, but simply read it. He was ecstatic.

"Who are you?" Literal asked the gentleman excitedly.

"Mustram Bertram Sumboddy," came the reply, "but my friends call me Muzz."

"Ah, Muzz B. Sumboddy, eh?" said Literal, sizing up the man with glee. "May I publish this story?"

"What, my boiler log?" asked Muzz. (Muzz worked as the boiler attendant at a suburban apartment complex, and the paper Literal had read was his ongoing log of boiler maintenance.)

"Is that the title? May I read it aloud?" Literal began orating sans answer:

August 27, 9 a.m. Pilot light checked. August 27, 10 a.m. Spiders cleaned out.

"I will make you famous," Literal prognostificatedly promised.

"Okay," said Muzz. "But I gotta be back at the boiler at noon."

What, My Boiler Log? was received with great acclaim, and Literal was now the father of the famous No-Metaphor literary movement, complete with his own protégé. Literal published several other books, including *Woman Makes Toast, Kids Are Swimming,* and his masterwork *I Will Cut the Grass Now.* He also continued to publish Muzz's boiler logs (Volume 27 of which was made into a film starring Robert DeNiro, James Woods, and the corpse of Phyllis Diller that swept all categories at the Oscars). With his success firmly entrenched, Literal began teaching a college course on the genre.

"No, no, no," he chastised a student one day, "you cannot write that the *hefty* woman was wearing a *tawdry* outfit. No adjectives! Adjectives are judgmental! Instead, *The woman was wearing an outfit.* How do you know what hefty and tawdry are? One woman's hefty is another woman's trim; one woman's tawdry is another woman's chic!"

"But," said the student "you just used an adjective,

'judgmental,' to describe adjectives after telling us not to be judgmental."

"No irony either!" shouted Literal. It was useless. No one could possibly hope to achieve success in the genre, for truly, no one had Literal's birth defect to guide them. Other authors instinctively infused meaning into their work, as well as adjectives, and gave up trying to become part of the genre in great despair. Thus, the college course was short-lived. Literal returned to his writing, authoring several more best-sellers, including his farewell piece *I Am Dying*. At Literal's jam-packed funeral, Muzz delivered a 3-word eulogy in homage to the man and genre, saying "He wrote books."

THE DUNG BEETLE REALIZES ITS POTENTIAL

"Same shit, different day," droned Routine, taking full ownership of his underachievement.

"You lucky bastard!" said the Dung Beetle, "...although I would argue that if it's the same shit and a different day, you're not being very efficient."

"No, you don't understand," said Routine. "It's just an expression. Human beings use the word 'shit' to represent the most undesirable aspects of existence."

"WHAT???!!!" exclaimed the Dung Beetle. "Do you mean to say that you use the staff of life, manna itself, God's gift to the Earth, as a catch phrase for *undesirable* things?"

The more the Dung Beetle thought about it, the angrier he became. He stamped around in high dudgeon in a small circle, leaving tiny poop prints, and muttering "Anarchist!"

"Don't you have a word you use to represent the most undesirable things in *your* existence?" asked Routine sympathetically.

"Yes, of course!" said the Dung Beetle.

"And what is it?" asked Routine.

"Love," said the Dung Beetle, his anger only somewhat abated.

"Well, you see, we're even then...love, for us, is the ultimate achievement."

The Dung Beetle could not believe his ears. "Oh, somebody fucking pinch me already," he said sarcastically, his anger again rising.

There was an awkward moment of silence during which Routine realized he was talking to a Dung Beetle and the Dung Beetle considered litigation. The Dung Beetle was the first to speak, offering an olive branch of sorts.

"Well, let me see this 'same shit' you're talking about."

"I'm telling you, it's not actual shit...it's not what you're thinking."

"Nonetheless," said the Dung Beetle. "I truly need to see whatever it is that you refer to as 'shit'."

Routine, eager to calm the Dung Beetle's frayed nerves, offered to take him to work to witness the shit firsthand. Routine had a horrible job not worth describing, and toiled within a windowless cubicle so drab that one could not describe it even if it were worth it. Routine brought the Dung Beetle into a 9 a.m. meeting with the CEO.

The CEO, whose fingernails gleamed from a $450 manicure, and whose watch alone was worth more than Routine's annual salary, addressed the entire company with smiles and lies preceding layoffs. The Dung Beetle watched, his mouth watering. In the middle of the CEO's speech, the Dung Beetle simply exclaimed "You're right! This is total shit!" and leapt upon the CEO, quickly rolling him into a ball, smaller and smaller, until all you could see of the former human was one astonished eye, pieces of a power tie, and the glint of a cell phone.

The employees issued the Dung Beetle a standing ovation. Routine was shocked.

"But, but..." he began, "That wasn't actual shit...how did you...why did you..."

"Oh, please," said the Dung Beetle. "That was *total* shit... show me more! Show me more!"

Routine took the Dung Beetle home, turned on the television, and handed him the remote. The Dung Beetle screamed with delight.

"Where is this person?" he demanded excitedly, referring to the televangelist on the screen.

"I dunno," said Routine, "maybe California...wait, there's an address for donations...he's in Ohio."

The Dung Beetle became silent suddenly, and shut his eyes tight. Routine could hear a slight hum emanating from his mandible. And then, as Routine glanced at the TV, the televangelist was toppled by a small army of Dung Beetles and rolled around the studio into a tiny ball.

"Whoa!" Routine yelped. "How did you...what did you...?!"

"Telepathy," said the Dung Beetle casually.

Routine watched in fascination as the Dung Beetle deployed his minions to deal with news anchors, bad sitcom stars, sports figures, self-appointed community leaders, talk show hosts, annoying home redecorators, even TV chefs. In a matter of 15 minutes the country was in crisis.

The Dung Beetle then leveled its gaze upon Routine, and approached him slowly.

"You're full of shit, too, aren't you?" he said slowly. "Nowhere job, cheating on your wife, blaming your failures on an alleged creator..."

"Now, wait a minute, buddy," said Routine, backing away, "I'm no different than anyone else..." In the millisecond after he made that statement, Routine knew he had signed humanity's death warrant.

"And to think we've been content dealing with the random

droppings of lesser animals...no more! No more!" The Dung Beetle quickened its pace toward Routine.

"WAIT!!! WAIT!!!" screamed Routine, "You want shit? You want real, unadulterated, 100% total shit?! I'll give you shit beyond your wildest dreams!!!"

The Dung Beetle, intrigued, stopped in his tracks. "Waddya got?" it asked menacingly with a hint of distrust.

Routine rushed to the TV and turned on the mind-numbing channel where a single camera rested upon the bloated, torpid, self-serving workings of Congress.

The Dung Beetle watched in fascination, his mouth a waterfall.

"What is *this*??!!" he demanded, mesmerized.

"The *government*," Routine said enticingly. "The biggest pile of shit you'll ever roll...and there's one or more in *every country*, one more full of shit than the next...make no mistake, my friend, this is the cream of the crap."

"Where is it?" demanded the Dung Beetle. Routine answered, and the next thing he knew he was driving the Dung Beetle at full throttle to Washington DC, the anticipatory drool of the Dung Beetle threatening to fill the car. During the ride, the Dung Beetle became silent, his mandible humming. When they arrived at The White House, it seemed that every Dung Beetle in the world must have been there...Routine gazed in fascination and horror at the sea of black exoskeletons, churning, writhing, 50 feet high...the Dung Beetle leapt from the car and joined the overwhelming throng as it moved as one toward the White House.

Had the event been televised, it would have garnered the most amazing ratings in history; however, the Dung Beetle army had laid waste to the whole of television (as well as print) journalism...only those present were witness to the surreal vision of the White House being toppled end over end by the Dung Beetle mass until it became a tiny ball, with only the President's genitals and John Hancock's signature from the Declaration of Independence visible.

Routine got into his car and gunned it, knowing that it was only a matter of time before the Dung Beetles had rolled the governments of the world into tiny balls and would come for him. He also knew that, because their taste for shit had been elevated to the extreme, that they would no longer be satisfied with the mere droppings of lesser animals. Resigned to his fate, Routine scraped and gathered as much scat as he could find, caked it onto himself, and spent the rest of his life hiding from the Dung Beetles in the only place he knew they would not bother to look: under a pile of common shit.

ME AND BILL ARE STILL PARTYIN'

Me and Bill used to party all the time, but then Bill moved to California, so we party by mail.

I roll a big joint, light it up, take a massive hit, put it out, and mail it to Bill. Bill gets it, lights it up, takes a massive hit, puts it out, and mails it back to me. And so on, until the roach is too little to smoke and somebody just eats it. Whoever eats it texts the other dude and says it's his turn to roll a fat one.

The downside is that me and Bill are never high at the same time, but it's the best thing we could think of to keep partyin' together.

TOUGH

"When the going gets tough, the tough get going," said Boss Coachy (just back from a Corporate Manager's Cliché Workshop) to his Corporate Team.

"Going *where*, though?" asked Sally. "Going away? Retreating? I never understood that saying."

"No, no, no!" said Boss Coachy, donning the fake smile he learned about in the Fake Smiles to Build Trust Workshop. (Boss Coachy had perfected his fake smile by wearing false teeth.) "They get going! They take action!"

"But how do we know if we're tough?" asked Sassy.

"Yeah," added Saggy, "I mean, if you expect this cliché to inspire us in a problem-solving capacity for more than 47 minutes, I think we'd need to have the basic personality traits that would enable us to truly 'get going.' Otherwise, your results will be dismal."

The company had a strict policy that any employee using the word "results" had to back up their claim with statistics, so Saggy immediately shared graphs, charts, a PowerPoint presentation, a symposium, a published proceedings of the symposium, and a 5-year return-on-investment study.

"Hmmm...compelling data, Saggy," said Boss Coachy. "Let's do a Life Examination Workshop right now to find out if we're tough. We'll take stock in ourselves...excuse me... that's my cell...hello?"

It was the stockholders.

"No, stock in *ourselves*, not company stock...yes, no worries... yes...goodbye." Boss Coachy returned his attention to his team. "Let's remember, team, that everything we say and do is being recorded, not only for surveillance purposes, but for the 24-hour reality TV show about us and everyone else in America."

"Yeah," said Sappy, "my favorite show is the show about the husband and wife who sit on the couch all day watching the show about themselves sitting on the couch all day watching the show about themselves."

The team agreed with Sappy and began chattering on about the show, saying stuff like "Did you see the one where..." and "That's the episode in which..." and so on. Boss Coachy turned on his Power Tie to get the group's attention.

"The workshop! The workshop!" he said, simultaneously adopting and losing patience. "Sally, let's start with you. Was there an experience in your life when the going got tough? And if so, did you get going?"

"Well," shared Sally, "one time my parents got divorced twice and fought over me and then didn't fight over me, and said bad words that hurt like punches and punched me."

"Excellent! I mean, not excellent, but what did you do?" said Boss Coachy, turning off his Power Tie to conserve energy and go green.

"I withdrew emotionally, painted disturbing pictures on my bedsheets with my feces, and began to randomly cut the flesh of my arms and buttocks with action figures."

Boss Coachy surreptitiously called Human Resources.

"I got the story on Sally's arms," he whispered, everyone hearing him. "I'll draft a memo later."

"Hmmm," said Boss Coachy, "it seems you didn't get tough and get going. Anyone else? Saggy?"

"Well," said Saggy, "to tell you the truth, nothing tough has ever happened to me. I hate tough things. I think everything in life should be nice and fluffy, like a bunny on a rainbow in love with sprinkles."

"Hmmm," said Boss Coachy thoughtfully, utilizing his skills from the Say Hmmm Thoughtfully to Stall for Time and Collect Your Thoughts Workshop. "Could you please go refill the water bottle, Saggy?"

"Certainly!" said Saggy in a Can-Do timbre. Boss Coachy

secretly activated the trap door by the water cooler that led to the Mailroom with everyone watching.

"Who else? Who else?"

"Well," began Sassy, "one time I was faced with a seemingly insurmountable situation that threatened to negate my entire model of reality."

"Yes? Yes? And what did you do?" asked Boss Coachy excitedly.

"I developed a proactive and strategic plan by thinking outside the box and ensuring that it synergized and dovetailed in a value-added manner."

"Excellent! Excellent! And what happened?"

"Well, the moment I attempted to enact the plan, I crumpled into the fetal position and cried out for my imaginary friend Icey Cream Angel."

Boss Coachy surreptitiously called Human Resources.

"I got the story why Sassy always cries 'Icey Cream Angel,'" he whispered, everyone hearing him. "I'll draft a memo later."

Boss Coachy was crestfallen. It seemed no one was tough. Only Sappy was left.

"How about you, Sappy?" asked Boss Coachy in a semi-defeated tone.

"I chewed harder," said Sappy, who subsequently shared that the only tough thing in her life had been a piece of steak gristle that she inadvertently began chewing because her butler Pukins had trimmed her T-Bone incorrectly.

"Is that true, or did you just say that for the TV show?" asked Boss Coachy.

"TV show," admitted Sappy. (Sappy was up for an Emmy for Best Supporting Asshole.)

"How about you, Boss Coachy? Are you tough?" asked the group in unison and 4-part harmony.

Boss Coachy had feared this question, and was dismayed that the How to Answer Questions You Fear Workshop was not until next month. Truth was, he was a leader who could not lead, a mentor without mentation, a True Stuporvisor.

In a moment of panic, Boss Coachy confused his learnings from the Lies and Truth Workshop with his take-aways from the Truth and Lies Workshop and inadvertently showed weakness to his team by being honest.

"I was only 27 when a group of thugs from the local Math Club attacked me," he said in a feeble voice, "they put a big shirt on me that had the face of a calculator printed on the front, and then they punched the numbers on the shirt calculator really hard with their fists until the answer was 6,704."

A moment of silence passed during which Boss Coachy sniffled and 3,405 adults around the world died of lung cancer.

"Ever since that day, I've been terrified of being around groups of more than 2 people, and I soil myself whenever I'm in that situation."

"So you're terrified right now 'cause you're with us, and we're a group of more than 2 people?" asked Sappy.

"Exactly," admitted Boss Coachy.

"And you're soiling yourself as we speak?" asked Sally.

"Like a threatened toad," said Boss Coachy sadly. "But thank God for these excellent adult diapers I get at Sam's Club."

Sappy surreptitiously called Human Resources.

"I got the story on that huge changing table in the men's room."

"*Now* what are we gonna do?" droned Sassy. "None of us is tough!"

"We'll just have to recruit someone onto the team that's tough," said Boss Coachy with sudden determination, "even though I know that increasing our numbers will terrify me and cause more soilage."

"Wow, that's kinda tough of you right there, Boss Coachy," said Sally.

"Not tough enough, you brown-noser," said Boss Coachy. "What we need is someone like...like...Clint Eastwood!"

"Yeah, right," said Sassy, all sarcastical-like. "And how the hell are we gonna get Clint Eastwood to join our team?"

"I couldn't help but overhear you," said Clint Eastwood, who had been under the conference room table. He crawled out from under the table and straightened himself up, killing a few beats while the producers sweetened the soundtrack with applause.

"We need a tough guy on our Corporate Team," said Boss Coachy. "None of us are tough, the going is getting tough, and we can't get going."

Clint sighed. "No can do," he said wistfully. "My recent work, both in front of and behind the camera, is more or less an apology for my earlier tough stuff. In the 1970s I was sardonically blowing criminal's faces off pre-trial in full rogue cop vigilante mode...now I'm making films about World War II from the perspective of the enemy. I'm not tough enough to get going. I'm not sure I ever was...in fact, I have no idea who I am."

Clint crawled back under the table.

"Yikes," said Boss Coachy, and then an idea hit him.

"John Wayne!" he exclaimed.

"John Wayne is dead," said Sally dryly.

"We'll dig him up!" Boss Coachy exclaimed.

"Exhume The Duke?" said Sally incredulously.

"Exactly!" said Boss Coachy. "The Duke's rotting corpse is probably tougher than any living, breathing man, I'll wager. Let's go, team!"

Exhuming John Wayne would have normally been out of the question, but it was sweeps month. Boss Coachy and his team stood around the Duke's grave site as the backhoe did its work. A crane lifted the coffin from its earthy niche, and the coffin was pried open with a crowbar.

The violent aroma of John Wayne's rotting carcass hit the group like an anvil up the nostril. They reeled back in aromatic horror. The Duke sat up.

"Whattsa matter, ya pansies?" he drawled. "Haven't ya ever smelled a long-dead man before?" A maggot crawled out from one of the Duke's eye sockets, slid across his face, and disappeared into one of his nostril holes, leaving a glistening trail of slime.

"Mr. Wayne," said Boss Coachy, approaching the coffin with a handkerchief over his nose, "we'd very much like you to join our Corporate Team. We're in desperate need of someone tough."

The Duke cocked his head in consideration of the request, which caused it to separate from his spine and roll into his lap. His rotten body then collapsed in a heap. Boss Coachy and his team waited a few moments for a reply, but it did not come.

"I think he's dead," said Boss Coachy. The coffin was re-sealed and lowered into the ground, and the backhoes replaced the dirt.

"Back to the drawing board," said Boss Coachy, heading for the office.

Boss Coachy and his Corporate Team, dejected, made their way back to the conference room, with Boss Coachy stopping by the men's room to be changed.

"Any ideas? Anyone?" asked Boss Coachy as they took their seats.

"Oh, triple DUH!" said Sappy. "I have a relative in God's Devils! He's a second cousin twice removed from our dinner parties because of lewd gesticulations. I'll call him. He's plenty tough."

"God's Devils, *the motorcycle gang*?" said Boss Coachy

shakily. He slowly rose from his seat and made his way back to the changing table.

Within 16 minutes, 15 members of God's Devils roared into the conference room, stacked vertically atop a single gas-electric-hybrid motorcycle. Yes, they were fierce, nasty, and terrifying, but they were green.

"Hello, Sappy," said Sappy's second cousin Dirt Bomb. "What can we do for you?"

"I'll let my supervisor tell you," said Sappy. She looked around for Boss Coachy, but he was nowhere in sight.

"Boss Coachy?" she called.

Boss Coachy entered the room slowly, his face pale and quaking with fear. Knowing that he would be unable to control his bodily functions in the face of such terror, but also knowing that he had a responsibility to upper management to be takin' care of bizzness (every day), he had immersed himself naked (save his Power Tie) into an empty 500-gallon aquarium, with holes cut in the bottom so that his legs stuck out and he could make his way around the room. He emptied himself forcefully from both front and back as he joined the group in the conference room.

"And who in God's Hell are you?" bellowed Twisto Jr., the biggest, hairiest, ugliest, baddest God's Devil since Twisto Sr. (who is now a priest with his own gardening show).

Boss Coachy's tank was instantly filled to the halfway mark.

"We need a tough guy to join our team to help solve a BCP," stammered Boss Coachy like the Tin Man in that scene where he's talking to the wizard with the flames shooting out and stuff.

"A BCP?!" yelled Twisto Jr.

"Big Corporate Problem," explained Sassy.

"Oh," grumbled Twisto Jr. "What's the situation?"

Boss Coachy's tank began to overflow, and he was forced to delegate the downloading and debriefing of the BCP to Sappy.

"No problem, Boss," said Sappy, and she asked the God's Devils to be seated while she brought up a PowerPoint presentation. Boss Coachy made his way out of the room as gingerly as he could, the products of his bowels and bladder making totally surfable waves in the tank with his every step.

Boss Coachy slowly made his way to the men's room (to his dismay, the cameras decided to follow him rather than remain in the conference room to capture the PowerPoint presentation debriefing download). With the glass cutter that he used to make his leg holes, he cut a 2-inch hole in the bottom of the tank, and positioned the hole over the toilet. He had just begun draining his personal cesspool when a knock at the stall door echoed through the executive washroom.

"You gonna be long?" a voice asked.

Boss Coachy simply looked at the camera, and the producers cued the giggle track.

Two hours later, the tank was dry, and Boss Coachy stepped out of it and into a fresh tank he had prepared (he had no choice; the God's Devils were probably still there). He returned to the conference room. To his surprise, only Sappy was present.

"Oh, hi Boss," said Sappy. She seemed disoriented, dazed.

"Sappy," said Boss Coachy, surprised to see her alone. "Where is everybody? Where are the God's Devils? What about the BCP?"

"BCP is solved," said Sappy. "God's Devils took care of it. Look at these results."

Sappy numbly brought up a PowerPoint presentation. Profits were through the roof. Productivity was through the roof. Morale was through the roof. Also through the roof was the head of the new company mascot, Necky the Giraffe, which the God's Devils had stolen from the local zoo.

"This is FANTASTIC and SUPER!" squealed Boss Coachy with glee. "How did they do it??"

"Murder, prostitution, counterfeiting, arson, and narcotics trafficking," drawled Sappy.

Boss Coachy was taken aback two steps. "Good Lord...where are Sassy and Sally?" he asked.

"Pushing dope and turning tricks," said Sappy.

Boss Coachy's flabber was totally gasted. "Where are the God's Devils now?" he asked with his mouth agape, rendering the question devoid of consonants.

"On their way to kill Carl Egbert Orifice."

"They're going to kill CEO?" yelped Boss Coachy in horror.

"...and take over the company...oh, *do* something, Boss Coachy!"

Boss Coachy knew he couldn't beat the God's Devils to CEO's office encumbered by a 500-gallon aquarium, so he shed the tank, steeled himself, and began sprinting to the office naked, Corporate Carpets be damned.

He overtook the vertically stacked motorcyclists in the hallway, which was not surprising, as the God's Devils had to drive extremely slowly so that no one fell off. Boss Coachy burst into Carl Egbert Orifice's office and slammed the door behind him.

"Ah, Coachy," said CEO. "Conserving clothing, I see. Is that part of this 'going green' thing? If so, bully for you and the planet! Hmmm...where's your diaper, Coachy? You're defecating on my putting green..."

"CEO, I need to tell you something urgently!" said Boss Coachy. The whiny, one-sixteenth-of-a-Harley sound of the hybrid motorcycle became audible in the background.

"Before you do, Coachy, tell me, have you made any progress on the BCP?"

"Well, you see, that's just it," said Boss Coachy hesitantly, "the problem is solved...everything is through the roof..."

"Yes! I saw the giraffe! Necky, right? Helluva giraffe. How'd you do it, Coachy?"

Louder approaching hybrid motorcycle.

"Well, sir, I subcontracted it, subdelegated it...but there's a problem..."

"Well, what is it, Coachy? Out with it, man!"

At that moment, CEO's door burst open and the God's Devils made their sluggish yet terrifying entrance. They clambered down from their motorcycle and surrounded CEO's desk. Boss Coachy, with nothing left to expel, excreted his internal organs and skeleton and crept cowering into the corner.

"This company is OURS!" screamed Dirt Bomb.

"I was supposed to say that," complained Twisto Jr.

"Whoops, my apologies...please," said Dirt Bomb.

"This company is OURS!" screamed Twisto Jr.

Twisto Jr. looked at Dirt Bomb. "Now you go ahead and say the next part."

"No, please," said Dirt Bomb. "I feel bad about before. You finish 'er up."

Twisto Jr. nodded at Dirt Bomb thankfully and turned back to CEO.

"If you get down on your hands and knees, drop yer pants, put this peacock feather in yer ass, and crawl out of here wearing this fancy blue bonnet and singing 'Itsy Bitsy Spider' in falsetto, we might not carve our credo into your back," bellowed Twisto Jr.

Dirt Bomb held up the peacock feather and fancy blue bonnet like Vanna White.

"What is our credo again?" asked Mudslide, new to the gang.

"We Love Our Hybrid Motorcycle, with a heart shape where the word 'love' is," said Twisto Jr.

"And after all that we're gonna kill ya anyway," piped up

Squeaky, who wouldn't even be in the gang except that he's Dirt Bomb's little brother and Dirt Bomb's Mom says Dirt Bomb has to watch him.

CEO rose slowly from his seat.

"Hasta la Vista, Baby, I'll Be Back, Make My Day, Life Is Like a Box of Choc-o-lates" he said evenly. To Boss Coachy's surprise, CEO proceeded to kick all the God's Devils' asses simultaneously by quickly and haphazardly sewing all their asses together, donning an extremely large boot, and executing an extremely exaggerated kick wind-up followed by the actual ass-kicking. The God's Devils flew through the roof upon impact, which confused Necky.

"That was amazing!" said Boss Coachy, swallowing his organs and skeleton, straightening himself up, and adjusting his Power Tie.

"Well, when the going gets tough, the tough get going, Coachy" said CEO with half a grin in order to conserve grin energy.

"You sure are tough!" said Boss Coachy, mesmerized like a kid meeting a bigger cooler kid. While staring at CEO in admiration, respect, and amazement, Boss Coachy saw a God's Devils pleather jacket on CEO's coat hook behind him by way of its reflection in the plate glass covering the framed photograph of CEO teeing off with Art Carney in 1982 that hung on the wall behind CEO's desk.

CEO looked Boss Coachy in the eye and began to laugh menacingly. "Will there be anything else, Coachy?" he cackled.

"No sir," said Boss Coachy, dazed.

"Then go fill the water bottle, will you boy?"

CEO secretly activated the trap door by the water cooler with everyone watching as Boss Coachy dragged himself out of CEO's office toward his demotion.

KNOCK KNOCK

Death, Opportunity, and the Avon Lady were all at my door at the same time. I didn't know what not to do. I'll admit I needed some facial cream, but I was too young to die. Opportunity, having knocked only once, stood by as Death rapped on the door with his scythe. The Avon Lady rang the bell.

I tiptoed out the back door and, disguised as a Girl Scout selling cookies, joined them on the front porch. The Avon Lady grew tired of waiting and tried to sell Death some hand lotion.

"Your hands are chapped and dry," she solicited, taking his skeletal appendage into her perfect palm, "perhaps you'd be interested in some lotion for them."

"Fuck off," said Death politely. Suddenly, Death turned and saw something that scared him to himself. He turned even more pale, his sunken eyes somehow bulged in terror, and he fled. The Avon Lady, also glancing back, was so horrified that she dropped all her merchandise. Her various creams, powders, and lipsticks spilled to the ground, forming an exact albeit surreal replica of Da Vinci's *The Last Supper*, but no one noticed. The terrified Avon rep screamed five-lungedly, leapt onto a horse that I hadn't noticed was there, and galloped away, kicking up more dust than a season's worth of slides. Even Opportunity had fled, but that was nothing new. I stood alone on the porch, terrified to even turn and glance at the unspeakable horror that had driven the unlikely combo from my door.

Taking a deep wavering breath into my quaking lungs, I spun around violently and laid my eyes upon the terror. My blood ran cold as Walt Disney.

I stood frozen as they joined me on the porch, ruffling their *Watchtowers* and rapping on the door. I then remembered that I was safe in my disguise...I'd just let them knock on the soon-to-be-unanswered door, and they'd go away!

"I guess they're not home," I said in mock prepubescent scout falsetto.

Suddenly, to my total shock, I answered the door, drove the Jehovah's Witnesses away by breathing fire, and bought ten boxes of cookies from myself.

"See?" said Opportunity, peeking out from behind a bush on the side of the porch, "*that* was the opportunity...to breathe fire and buy cookies from yourself!"

Both of myselves looked in disgust at Opportunity, and began pelting him with Thin Mints until he was rendered a landscape of bruises, welts, and contusions.

LIFE IS FAIR

PEE FACE: Who ever said life was fair?

RAT FACE: Donald J. Bloodroid, that's who.

DONALD J. BLOODROID: That's true, I did say it, and I'll say it again, but not at this moment; perhaps later. I remember when life was fair. I smoked 300 cigarettes a day and ate all the fat off a cow, and it took 5 years off my life, but it was fair; it was taken off the *end* of my life. Could you imagine how unfair it would have been if those 5 years were taken from the middle of my life?

PEE FACE: Life gives me half of everything it has. I'd say that's pretty fair.

RAT FACE: It gives you half a breath of air? Who gets the other half?

PEE FACE: Death. I breathe in order to live, but each breath I take propels me that much closer to death.

DONALD J. BLOODROID: Turtles live 150 years because they breathe really slowly.

PEE FACE: I'd breathe slow if I moved slow like a slow-breathing, slow-moving turtle.

DONALD J. BLOODROID: Let's try it. Let's move and breathe like turtles.

150 years later...

DONALD J. BLOODROID: It worked.

PEE FACE: And Rat Face has laid 50,000 eggs.

BIRTHDAY LAWSUIT

The woman had just been raped. It was her birthday. She sat in the police station without presents, looking like a vampiress from tears and black eyeliner. Her shirt was ripped, and the parts of it intact covered more bruises.

A cup of coffee and policeman sat gently next to her and produced a clean horror sheet.

"Can you describe the assailant at all, ma'am?" came more gentleness.

"It was dark," the shaken human staticked, "I was wearing a ski mask..."

"Ma'am?"

"He...he was wearing a ski mask...(vocal aftersob)...(clearing)...He was a white man, wearing all black, about 5 foot 11...that's it..."

"Ma'am, did he have any identifiable scars or features?"

The woman sniffed snobs and thought. A light with legs sprang into her eyes.

"Yes...yes!...He had a nose ring with two birds tied to it with string..."

"Were the birds bound to the ring, or were they able to fly about?"

"They were tied by one leg with about three feet of string... they flew about."

"Ma'am, what type of birds were they?"

"Type of birds?...Oh, God, I don't remember!"

The woman began to sob into her filthy hands, and the sergeant dispatched four cars to ready a line-up.

The line-up was assembled. The horrified woman sat down in front of the bizarre theater, not looking up at all.

"Ma'am, each one of these men will step forward for a moment. I want you to identify the assailant when you see him. Number one!"

A man stepped from shadow into spotlight.

"No," stammered the woman, almost relieved, "the birds were much smaller than that."

"Number two!"

Mug replaced mug.

"No, that's Merv Griffin."

"Number three!"

The accused stepped forward. He was juggling.

"It couldn't have been him. He couldn't have raped me while juggling," sobbed the woman.

"Could so have," muttered three, his professionalism insulted. He was silenced by the police immediately with a "sshhh" and billy club to the throat.

"Number four!"

A white man, 5 foot 11, wearing all black, a ski mask, and a nose ring with two birds attached to it stepped into the light. The woman gasped and shook a shaky finger.

"That's him," she underexploded, "that's him!"

The accused pulled off his ski mask. It was her husband. Balloons and confetti fell from the ceiling.

"SURPRISE!" shouted everyone.

HIS WORK WAS REJECTED AGAIN AND AGAIN; WHY, OH, WHY, GOD DAMN IT?

His work was rejected again and again; why, oh, why, God damn it? Perhaps it was because the opening lines of his stories were simply repeats of the titles. Some publishers were cruel:

Dear Mr. Wood:

Thanks you for your submission; we love your novel and would very much like to publish it.

Just kidding. It was trite, unimaginative, and derivative of other bad writing.

Just kidding. We love your novel and would very much like to publish it.

Again, kidding.

Worst,

Beaver Press

And another:

> *Dear Mr. Wood:*
>
> *Fuck.*
>
> *PS: You.*
>
> *No regards,*
>
> *Woodchuck Books*

In desperation, he committed suicide, hoping against hope and betting against bet that his work would be published posthumously. When no one noticed his suicide, he repeated it, this time killing the President before he took his own life. In 100 years, his work had not yet appeared in print; even the news articles regarding his assassination of the President did not mention him by name, and simply read "An unknown and unpublished author killed the President today."

Out of ideas, he realized that the goal, after all, was to maintain complete artistic control over one's work, and that the pure joy of the creative process was the true reward of writing. Just as he finally convinced himself of this, the noted author T. Booligan Cranewoothy sped by in his flame orange Roustabout convertible, baring his three testicles and shouting "You're wrong."

He settled on vanity publishing, and his work remained in the top drawer of his vanity until the maid inadvertently set the vanity on fire with her mind.

HOLY ALE

Religion A was fighting Religion B on behalf of God and vice versa. Each of their Gods was on their side, and their respective ancient Holy Books assured them that, should the battle become too messy, their God would intervene on their behalf and decimate the enemy.

The nonbelievers stood by drinking beer, horrified at the irony that humankind would destroy itself in an attempt to curry favor with an alleged creator.

"Also hogtied into the mix is the irony that the remains of one extinct race, dinosaurs, will contribute to the extinction of another, because of, you know, fighting for oil," said the nonbelievers, opening another beer.

Yes, the holy war had an oil subtext, because we need oil to help run the lawnmower, and damn that grass is getting high.

"I am so sorry," wrote T-Rex in a public letter of apology as early as 1972, "I did not intend to turn into oil...had I known the trouble it would cause, I would have turned into crap."

"More irony, fit for another beer," said the nonbelievers, reading aloud a crumpled copy of T-Rex's letter that one of them kept in his wallet next to his decaying condom, "even if T-Rex turned to crap, we would still fight over it. Tyrants, kings, and leaders would have palaces built on crap profits, and instead of raping the citizenry through taxes, they would demand that two-thirds of every bowel movement be mailed to the government by April 15."

"That's worth 2 beers right there," said the nonbelievers.

Double-fisted, the nonbelievers watched as Religion A waged its "Convert or Kill" campaign against Religion B's "You're Going to Hell and We're Not" effort.

To everyone's surprise (even the members of Religions A and B), two figures descended from the sky and began fighting with each other. It wasn't long before everyone realized that these two beings didn't know how to fight...they simply slapped at each other and chased each other around. After witnessing this for approximately 74 seconds, the religious returned to their war effort, and the nonbelievers to their beer.

"Is that God?" one nonbeliever asked, "I mean, are those God? You know what I mean."

"Join the army if that's what you think. We're nonbelievers, Goddammit. Those beings are obviously extraterrestrials."

"Wow, how will this end?" said a nonbeliever drinking Bud Ice.

"Perhaps an even-supremer being will stop the fight between the supreme beings," offered a nonbeliever nursing a Corona Extra.

"Lame," said another with a Mickey's Big Mouth almost at his lips, "that's like the Star Trek episode with Tremaine."

"Yeah, but how many people saw that?"

"That's not the point. It's a matter of artistic integrity. You can't just cop out and swipe somebody else's ending."

"Then how will it end?"

"I'm thinking, I'm thinking..."

Cries of "My God! My Lord!" and "Hit Him With the Left!" abounded from the battlefield, and in the next instant the two beings merged into one being, which happened to be a male toddler wearing only a diaper. The toddler produced two nukes, and tossed them to either side of the battlefield, destroying both armies. He then approached the nonbelievers.

"Are you God?" said a nonbeliever with two Molson Goldens.

"Shut up," said the toddler. "I thought you were supposed to be a nonbeliever."

"Even nonbelievers are desperate for some sort of understanding."

"Isn't it enough," said the toddler "that you understand that you need to approach a frog slowly if you want to observe it; that Wynonie Harris is the greatest of the blues shouters; that the ocean is excellent?"

"Will we find stuff out after we die?" said a nonbeliever drinking, to the dismay of his cohorts, O'Douls Amber.

"Why don't you find out why you're such assholes to each other while alive," snapped the toddler, his diaper suddenly turning into a pair of vintage Bermuda shorts in a miniscule display of his meaningless power.

"We're not assholes," grumbled a nonbeliever.

"Well, granted, you're not as bad as the dickstains I just wasted, but you're no angels either."

"Angels! You said angels!" said a teetering nonbeliever. "Are there angels?"

"Will you jackoffs stop hanging on my every word?" yelled the toddler, "I know about as much as you do. Jesus Christ!"

"You said Jesus Christ! Is there a Jesus? Was there a Jesus?"

"Oh, go to hell, all of you!" screamed the toddler.

"Hell! Hell! Is there a hell?"

"Will we find junk out after we die?" asked a nonbeliever

who had not been paying attention. The toddler, annoyed, drew a deep breath.

"What, this isn't good enough for you?" he exhaled, trying to remain patient. "Can you please just enjoy the fucking crackerjacks and forget about the prize? And would somebody remember their manners and get me a fucking beer?"

"But you're a toddler...can I see some ID?"

"Toddler, my ass! Did you see me descend from the sky as two beings, engage in an intentionally silly slap fight, merge into my current self, and get rid of those dickstains? ID, my ass! What're you guys drinking?"

"Uh...we got Bud, Bud Ice, Corona, Mickey's, Molson..."

"Swill! Swill!" shouted the toddler. He looked around. "You don't even have lime for the Corona!"

"Damn," said a nonbeliever with a Corona, "forgot the lime..."

"You guys are hopeless. Here..."

The toddler toddled over to a 1949 Mercury that no one had noticed was there and popped the trunk. He climbed into the trunk and began to hand case after case of beer to the nonbelievers.

"Holy Ale, huh?" said a nonbeliever, reading the type on the unopened case and discarding his Bud Ice. "Is it good?"

"Is it good," repeated the toddler mockingly, "drink it and find out, jackass!"

The nonbelievers discarded their current brews and began to swig the Holy Ale.

"Excellent!" they all shouted. "And what a buzz from one swig!"

"Damn straight," said the toddler, entering and revving up the 49 Merc and slowly rolling away. "This shit'll kick your ass."

"Where can we get more?" shouted the nonbelievers.

"Just look at the sky and ask me," said the toddler, "My name's Mel. Speak loud, I don't hear so good. Been in a band too long and was too macho to use earplugs."

The nonbelievers drank many beers that day in light of the final crushing irony that they would soon be waging war against the drinkers of inferior beers in the name of Mel.

TINY PARTS

My Dad's on the other side now, with his buddy Gil Patrick. Both Dad and his buddy Gil Patrick wound up obese, but Dad was the one to have the heart attack. Mr. Patrick sneezed one day in front of the TV and his nose started bleeding and didn't stop. My brother Gary and I went to the hospital to donate blood for Mr. Patrick, and I had an appointment to donate bone marrow but it was too late.

I remember the first time I met Mr. Patrick, which is to say I have the gist of a memory. My memory isn't like a memory at all; instead of really remembering things, some guy in my head tells me about what happened, and he heard it from someone else or read it somewhere. Along the way, he shows me some pictures, which don't really have anything to do with the overall memory, but instead capture seemingly insignificant details.

It was raining. For whatever reason my father was in charge of me that day, and he had to go to work. I guess he could have kept me busy picking up nails if it was sunny, but it wasn't. So he took me to his buddy Gil Patrick's electric shop and asked could Gil keep me busy, did Gil need a helper. Mr. Patrick was very happy to meet me and told my Dad yes he had a job for me. Off went my Dad, and Mr. Patrick brought me to the back of his electric shop, where there were about 5 aisles of never-ending metal shelves filled with countless glass jars containing the tiny parts necessary for an electrician to complete this or that and make something either light up or run.

Mr. Patrick explained to me that he needed me to pick up all the tiny parts that were strewn all over the floor, then find the jar on the shelf meant to contain the tiny part, and put the tiny part back in the jar. The room was poorly lit. He went back into the well lit paneled front office, and I heard him pour coffee.

I began my task. The rain beat steadily on the corrugated roof of the back of his electric shop. I picked up a tiny part, and looked up at the dizzying array of jars. I wasn't able to put but one or two tiny parts back.

I remember being overwhelmed and frustrated, and then giving up. I felt bad because I'd failed, and was nervous that I'd be back the next day and the day after that, until I'd finished. What did I know? I thought the job really needed doing. No one cared.

In retrospect I know that I was a little kid and that Dad couldn't watch me and work at the same time and that Mr. Patrick didn't have a job for me but had a way to keep me busy for 9 hours until my Dad got back. When Dad did get back, I said goodbye to Mr. Patrick and hopped into my

Dad's truck, a released prisoner.

I don't know how Dad and Mr. Patrick met, but I guess it was on some job. Dad was a master carpenter and Mr. Patrick an electrician, so I guess at some point Mr. Patrick gave power to one of my Dad's creations. Dad worked word-of-mouth building custom homes until the assembly line shithole mansions started popping up everywhere, at which point he went to work for a company that didn't know from craftsmanship and hated it. He used to tell me when I went to work with him that it was a wonderful life, and that the first order of business when he got to the job was to have a cup of tea. (On one occasion he said "life is great if you don't weaken," to which I responded "life is great on the weekends," and he laughed.) He loved being his own boss, and worked himself hard. When he retired early at 62 (unable to stand the boss of the shithole mansion company who couldn't tell a hammer from a calculator), his knees and shoulders were shot, and he settled in a one-stoplight town in Georgia with no restaurants to be near his brother. When he and his brother stopped speaking after 2 years because of my uncle's crazy shrew bitch of a wife, he slept, ate, grew too large to get his mail, and died. The last time I saw him, which was a month before he died, he told me he was tired of living. I told him that I was too. I was 35.

Mr. Patrick entrusted his electrical business to a young gift-of-gabber he met while in his late fifties who drove the business and Mr. Patrick's reputation into the ground within a year. Mr. Patrick, wide-eyed and ruined, was trying to figure out how to keep the house he'd lived in for the past 20 years when he sneezed the sneeze that led to his cancer diagnosis.

Mr. Patrick was religious, and so was my Dad, although Mr. Patrick believed the Bible verbatim while my Dad enjoyed the role of the biblical scholar with many questions. My Dad believed that God wanted us to ask questions, and not just lean on the Bible and close our minds. I hope he was right. I used to listen to Dad and Gil Patrick debate religion on the rare occasions that the three of us found ourselves in the same space. They talked a lot about the "apostle that Jesus loved." Mr. Patrick told my Dad without a trace of doubt or hesitation that it was Peter, and my Dad said it was Judas, because Jesus knew that Judas was predestined to be the heavy. "That's interesting, Woody," Mr. Patrick said without any inclination of changing his vote for Peter.

I was glad that my Dad had a friend like Mr. Patrick. I didn't see my Dad with any real friends, I guess because he had 6 kids, which didn't leave a lot of time for socializing. Toward the end of my Dad's life, when he was in Georgia and Gil Patrick was still in New Jersey, I didn't hear him talk about religion with anyone, and I wonder what Gil Patrick thought of the Bible toward the end. Probably a whole lot but maybe very little.

I guess everyone's life story has a sad ending because we all die, but we all do much more than that as we grow old. We watch friends die, we get divorced or watch our spouse die, we lose jobs, or accept a cascade of occupations denoting fewer and fewer of our original intentions. We lose touch with our kids if we had kids, they complain behind our backs that we're a pain in the ass. Sometimes the world will step in and trounce us, or disease will step in and do the same. And while we're winding down in so many ways, we can't hear, see, perceive, or react to the things happening to us as we would have in our youth, when we were fit to fight what converged upon us. Unless we're extremely lucky, life pours more and more cement mix into our hearts.

For all the tiny parts strewn on the floor that rainy day, I'm still sad that only a few made it back to their jars.

HOW HE DUMPED HER

HER: The bastard started taking me for Grant. Teasing me about being in the Civil War and shit.

SHE: Mine was worse. He took me for granite.

HER: Yeah?

SHE: Yeah. Built a fucking porch out of me. Then he started walking all over me.

HER: No!

SHE: Yeah. Five years later he put in a new porch. He tore me up, put me in a wheelbarrow, and dumped me.

HER: He dumped you?

SHE: Yeah.

HER: Did he have a father?

SHE: No.

HER: The bastard dumped you.

SHE: And he fucked me.

HER: The fucking bastard.

LARRY, GOD, AND EDISON IN THE SAME ROOM

Larry hated himself for his narcissism. He drank heavily to forget that he was an alcoholic. He held down a job with both hands, but it kept slipping through his fingers and hitting him in the brain.

"Why don't you get a real job, stop drinking, and stop loving/hating yourself?" asked his wife without question mark as she made love to his best friend who owed him three hundred dollars.

"What ever happened to the girl I married?" wondered Larry after he chopped his wife to bits, burned her remains, and completely forgot about the incident. Both Alzheimer's and alcoholism ran in Larry's family; at any given moment he would either drink to forget or forget to drink.

Things were back to normal. Larry sighed heavily, sucking in the entire room, and rearranged the furniture upon exhaling.

"Who invented the light bulb?" shouted Larry's future illegitimate son from an unknown womb, getting a jump on his inevitable homework.

"Thomas, Eddy's son," Larry replied to the worst of his knowledge. Thomas Edison then glided into the room without moving his feet.

"It's easy to invent things in heaven," Edison said happily. Suddenly his face twisted with pain. "Why did electronic music downloads ever replace the wax cylinder?" he moaned. He was cheered up again upon hearing that his original recording of "Mary Had a Little Lamb" was still in the Billboard top twenty.

Edison began looking in all the closets to make sure God was not in the room.

"Let me tell you something about God," said Edison, "he didn't really invent everything...he just realized the commercial possibilities."

"You're just saying that because that's what *you* did," said God, jumping out of the one closet Edison had failed to check.

"Wow," thought Larry, "Thomas Edison and God in the same room! I've got to get my camera." He searched in vain for his camera, but could only find a courtroom sketch artist. By the time he got back, God and Thomas Edison were cutting a remake of "I Got You Babe" on wax cylinder and had locked the door.

Larry, locked out of his own room and missing his wife and camera, signed a prenuptial agreement with his new lover stating that they would never be married.

SLEEPWORKING

Lately I've been sleepworking.

It starts out highly ironic: In the dead of night, I hit SNOOZE about 5 times, "get up" (as it were) for an unconscious shit, shower, and shave, somehow sleep through 5 cups of coffee, and am then dead to the world at 75 mph on the Jersey Turnpike toward my job.

I found out about my sleepworking when I left myself a memo. I'd been troubled by the fact that I'd arrive at my desk in the morning to find all of my work already done. Looking busy all day when you have no work is an art form, and the stress eventually gives you testicular cysts.

Could McHaid be after my job, I paranoi'd? Is he doing my job *and* his to prove to Biggy Boss Boy that I'm Unemployee of the Month? I approached McHaid, who denied my suspicions emphatically (he has always been overweight), but confided that it *was* a good idea, and asked if I would mind if he actually did it to me. I told McHaid I'd get back to him, and fled.

I returned to my office baffled, disoriented, paranoid,

alienated, and confused. Luckily, it was lunch time.

I went to Zazzy's and ordered a Double Stanko (Beeline Zazzy, owner of Zazzy's, had created the Double Stanko [a drink in which you eat a bottle of rum whole, throw yourself out a window, trudge back up the stairs and spit out the broken glass] when I complained that the original Stanko [15 consecutive shots of tequila consumed while already drunk on grain] had lost its bite). I confided my crazy problem to Larfly, Zazzy's deaf bartender. He was the only one I could trust besides the guy who plays "Floyd" on *The Andy Griffith Show*.

He listened intently (he was always fond of camping), and when I was through with my tale, he proclaimed, exactly like a deaf Clint Eastwood:

"Ya Been Sleepworkin,' Boy."

"W-W-*WHAT*?" I berserkled, frothing at the anus, "are you out of your element? Are you court jesting me? Have you completely lost your Mein Kampf over matter??!"

Larfly gave me another Double Stanko and told me the tale of how Zazzy himself had built the whole business in his sleep. Thought he was unemployed during the day; couldn't figure out where the money was coming from. It didn't hit him until he tried to take a nap at work and realized he was already asleep.

My eyes lit up, not in realization, but in two Double Stankos.

I thanked Larfly profusely, forgot to pay him, and returned to work. Sleepworking? It was crazy. I couldn't believe it. I needed proof. Before I left work that day, I left myself a memo. It read thusly:

Big Bobby's Balloon Company Memo

12/12/25
To: Life Jones
Frum: Life Jones
Re: Sleepwerking

Life:

Have you ben sleepwerking? Get bak to me on this ASP.

Life

The next day, as I approached my desk, I was in a cold sweat. I could see that my memo had been answered; my original memo was now underneath a new memo; a memo written by a nocturnal me. I prepared myself for complete weirdness, for bizarre feces, for surreal potato land face hole, for dreamy creamy terrorification, for a bumpy rickshaw ride to retardo. I knew it would be life altering, so I had my friend Devlin film it. We watch the film now and then.

INT: Life Jones approaches desk, looking at camera.

LIFE (addressing camera): Now we'll find out.

Life picks up memo and reads.

LIFE: "Life: Yes, I've been sleepworking. Life." Devlin, look at this memo. This is F'ing unbelievable.

DEVLIN: What, that you're sleepworking?

LIFE: No...no typos when I'm asleep...

Life's boss, Mr. Blastoff, enters the room corporately. He acknowledges camera in puzzlement, and addresses Jones.

MR. BLASTOFF: Jones, your work lately has been phenomenal. Not only have you saved the company, built a better mousetrap, and improved the wheel, but you've submitted a working cure for toe cancer and have re-filled the water bottle. From now on, you are Mr. Blastoff, and I am Goofbody G. Babyboy, Assistant to the Janitor's Assistant. Congratulations!

MR. BLASTOFF exits the office backwards, putting on 5 suits simultaneously and playing the trombone badly.

It was then that I knew I had to continue sleepworking. It was also then that Devlin ran out of film. To this day I'm sleepworking, and I now own two yachts and three oceans. My only dilemma is when I have insomnia and have to call in sick to work.

FEAR AND SCARINESS

Man wakes up in his bedroom to find a demon standing in the corner.

MAN: Whoa! Someone or something is really testing my model of reality. If this is a hallucination, caused by God knows what, maybe I should worry more about the cause of the hallucination than the hallucination itself, that is, if this really *is* a hallucination. It may just be real, and if it *is* real, I won't even know what "real" is anymore. Hmmm...well, I guess my first step is to determine whether it's physically here.

Man gets out of bed and walks toward demon.

MAN: If this is a hallucination, my hand will probably pass right through it, unless it's some sort of energy being, whereupon my hand may pass right through it and it still may be real.

Man stops in front of demon, attempts to pass his hand through, and it stops with a thud on the demon's shoulder.

MAN: Okay, neither of those two things. It seems to have

mass, to be here. Wow. My model of reality is really being tested...unless I'm hallucinating that I can actually touch it...I could be hallucinating strongly enough to simulate tactile as well as visual information...

Demon rips off man's arm and begins chewing it. Blood pours from man.

MAN: This is either the most horrifying experience anyone could ever have or the most complete hallucination. There has to be some flaw in this image, or I'm going to have to accept it as real and add it, albeit clashing, to my model of reality.

Demon rips out man's leg and begins to devour it.

MAN: All right, now there's something to think about. My leg is or seems to be gone. I'm getting the feeling, or, ironically, lack thereof, that it's actually gone, and so is my arm. Pain this intense can't be simulated, or can it? We know so little about the brain...maybe I'm using the other nine-tenths of my brain right now. God. So many questions.

Demon bolts upright in bed, horrified. He wakes his wife as well by his sudden jolt from sleep. She rolls over to see if he's okay.

DEMON (settling): Am I scary?

DEMON'S WIFE: Of course you're scary. Go back to sleep.

BEDTIME STORY FOR JACK

"To ruin a phrase," said Twinthy, "if it weren't for bad luck, I'd have no bad luck at all."

Truth, Bea told. Twinthy McBeautiful had the worst luck in the neighborhood. I remember when he hit the Pick-6 for 75 million the day of the second coming of Christ. He ripped up the ticket and combed his hair for Judgment, only to find that it was just a dress rehearsal. A dry run. A nothing burger. A brick lodged in the Secretary of the Treasury's lower intestine. A bad remake of *Happy Days* with a parrot as The Fonz.

He did manage to marry, but found out on his honeymoon that his wife had only married him because he had good records. He impregnated her while she wasn't looking, and, as no luck would have it, she died during childbirth. They decided then and there not to have any more kids.

"It's not so bad," chirped Badsmell, who was hired by the government to be Twinthy's friend, "my wife was dead not only after childbirth but throughout our marriage."

"But you're a necrophiliac," said Twinthy.

"Say that again and I'll kill you and make love to you," threatened Badsmell, who subsequently followed a duck out of the room and directly into the machine gun fire of a drug cartel picnic.

The day after the death/birth, Twinthy went to the hospital to bring his child a bosom full of milk. He knew his own wrong-sexed and arid breasts would not satisfy the tot's libido, so he had a partial sex change, rendering only his bosoms womanly.

The nurse pointed out Twinthy's child through the large glass window that looked into the hospital nursery. Twinthy was shocked.

"Why does my child have a horn?" he screamed softly.

The nurse explained the phenomenon. Twinthy was again shocked. He had not even noticed that his wife was a rhinoceros. He took the child and bounced it on his knee, the floor, and eventually went out to the park and shot a few baskets with it. After he had lost to himself in a game of 3-court one-on-one, he took the child in his arms and said softly, "You probably won't understand this, and you'll probably grow up thinking that I blame *you*, but you killed my wife."

"What'dya think, I was born yesterday?" the tyke screeched. She jumped out of his arms, did a shot of Wild Turkey, and screamed for a breast milk chaser.

Twinthy unzipped his horse costume and said, "Yes, I will breastfeed you, my demon seed." In three seconds, the child had bitten off and swallowed both breasts.

"The first thing you must learn, my offshoot," said Twinthy, now boasting the world's fastest double mastectomy, "is the definition of 'breastfeeding'."

The child suddenly grew ill and died. Twinthy blamed himself, for he had poisoned it. He left the corpse at the basketball court, taking only the horn to begin a scrimshaw hobby.

And now Twinthy had no wife, no child, and not enough funds to purchase the proper tools for scrimshaw. He pondered suicide. Should he kill himself? Would he get away with it? If he could do it quickly, get rid of the body, and leave the country immediately he might have a chance. He purchased a one-way plane ticket to Ulan Bator that night, and, slipping on a pair of gloves, snuck up behind himself in strangle mode. At the last minute he turned around, and a high-speed chase ensued. He ran straight to the police, and they locked him up for attempted murder. Twinthy was given life, but only wound up serving 3 days because his grammar was horrible and he could not finish his sentence.

Twinthy thought about his life and all that had happened to him. He summed it all up by saying to no one, "When you lose your job at the unemployment agency, you still have to go to work."

POSTURE

Belt slapped Cloud on the back no-reasonedly and started to pour beer into a cup he imagined was in his hands and onto the floor.

"You're drunk," said Cloud for everyone. They all threw Belt out (for no one at the party was sober enough to drive him home) and continued their drinking.

"I don't need them," alcoholed Belt, "I'll drive myself home drunk."

He knew he was in no condition to drive, so he ate breath mints and put on his sunglasses. He pulled out of the driveway sideways and hit a policeman, who had temporarily stepped out of his vehicle to collect dust.

The policeman, Redd Well, was not injured; nay, the accident in fact had cured the spinal disorder he had met at birth, and for the first time in his life, he was standing up straight.

"Even though I owe you my very life I still have to arrest you because you're really drunk. Can I have a breath mint?" said the cured policeman. Officer Well slapped the cuffs on

Belt, which made it difficult for him to retrieve the breath mint from his pocket. It was the very last mint in the roll, and was covered in lint. This angered the policeman; he threw Belt into the back of the squad car like midget tossing. Belt wanted to recite the alphabet to prove his non-existent sobriety, but could not remember the melody. He entertained the thought of trying to walk a straight line, but was afraid to do so without a net. As far as Belt knew, three identical officers were arresting him.

Redd slammed the door behind Belt and got in behind the wheel. He sent a message on thin air and received others. He put the car in drive and rolled from the scene. It was the scariest car Belt had ever been in, except for his own as he tried to drive it minutes ago...*minutes ago*. Belt felt regret, and laughed. Thank God he was still bombed, or he would start to be able to think.

Redd sat up straight. This and only this was the reason Redd Well was born again. He was sitting up straight. The doctors weren't just trying to cheer him up. He was six foot. The world looked completely the same from a different angle, and Redd could now fire his obnoxious tailor. He was going to buy regular clothes now, like, maybe that wormskin jacket with the girls on it. He was going to put the candy rooster atop the garage on Grandpa's birthday. He was going to...he was going to...*dance*.

Redd saw it coming up in the distance, and adrenaline tinged with revenge ran up and down his new spine. It blinked on and off, as it always did, but this time it did not taunt. This time it invited, almost challenged him. Redd was going to dance.

Belt was sober enough to lift his head and see the blinking neon sign that screamed "Van Gogh Go." He had been there to drink just that night. Had he gone back in time?

The concept – hang wall-sized repros of Van Gogh's classics, put them under strobe light, and animate them to music (heavy metal) with computer lasers. Put a dance floor down in the shape of a severed ear, not directly centered, but one inch out to the left, so that it is bizarrely unnerving. Animate the dance floor to emulate the swirling stars of *Starry Night*, and animate the people by giving each customer portrait lighting. Van Gogh Go. Redd slammed the car door behind him and trudged up the gravel parkway that surrounded the club.

Belt wasn't that stupid. As soon as Redd entered the club he fell out of the automobile and crawled away. He was very drunk. It seemed that his last half pint of Beelzebub Red was just starting to kick in. He felt 9.7% better as he crawled past all the gravel and onto clear pavement. He readied his circuits to stand. With cuffed hands, he balanced himself, trying to control his legs, which were as useless as white crayons. They wobbled and jerked like an epileptic Elvis, and his eyes, embarrassed for lack of information, looked away. It was all up to the legs, inertia, and God's mood. Belt stood for five seconds when he realized he had to now walk, and fell back down and continued crawling.

Redd was dancing. He was the only one there (how was Redd to know it was a club despised by all?), but he was dancing. He did the Freddie. He did the Pony. He did the Harlem Shuffle and the Limbo Rock. He did the Swim, the Fly, the Wiggle Wobble, the Duck, the Boogaloo, the Shingaling, the Funky Broadway, the Bristol Stomp, the Cool Jerk, the Fish, the Mashed Potato, the Watusi, the Loco-Motion, the Twist, the Madison, the Frug, the Monkey, the Hulley Gulley, the Walk, the Stomp, and the Dip. He made up some of his own dances, too, although clearly derivative of the aforementioned. The owner left Redd the keys and stabbed himself. Redd left the club dancing on air, for he had worn out the dance floor. He glided into the parking lot and picked up Belt, who was crawling in circles ten yards from the car.

"I feel great," Redd confided in Belt, "I was dancing."

"I feel like death," Belt belched, "my knees and palms are full of rocks."

Belt was amazed. He had spoken. For the first time in his life, he had clearly spoken in a complete drunken stupor. What had he said?

Redd helped Belt walk into the police station. It bothered him, for he wanted to glide up the stairs like an escalator, and he had to help Belt walk. "The hell with it," he thought, dropping Belt. He danced up the stairs slowly like a backward Bojangles, with Belt crawling behind him.

Redd's fellow officers were amazed at the new Redd. They stood around him bug-eyed and gulped. They did this, and Redd ate it up, for over two hours. By the time Redd brought the alcohol test for Belt, the alcohol had left his blood stream and he was sitting in a pond of his own urine, smiling.

"Breathe into this," Redd commanded the wet Belt. Belt obeyed. The breathalizer registered nothing.

"If he isn't drunk, he's on drugs!" Redd adopted. "Get a urine sample!"

Another officer appeared with a cloud-white plastic canister, and told Belt to pee in it. All the policeman turned their heads.

"But I don't have to pee anymore," exelched Belt, pointing to the janitors and surfers battling his urine pond.

"Then drink this," offered Redd, handing Belt a glass of grain alcohol.

Belt drank it down, and Redd brought back the breathalizer and busted him. Redd escorted Belt to a cell, thanked him for curing his spine, and shuffled off to Buffalo.

WHO SAYS RELIGION AND SCIENCE CAN'T CO-EXIST?

Religion is the manifestation of humanity's inability to accept that some questions don't have answers.

This does not exclude a creator; there very well may be one. I speak only of religion: the sects organized in order to worship a god or gods. Anyone on earth who pretends that they are sure there is a creator is, well, pretending or deluded. He/she does not have knowledge, but a belief. She/he may equate the two, but she/he/it is only human.

So, science moves forward, hypothesizing, testing, proving, disproving, and discovering while religion stays put in its individual and collective belief and is modified slightly based on societal pressures.

At its worse, religion becomes divisive, corrupted, and a convenient excuse to wage war. And science, ironically, provides the weapons.

HELLO, JOHN

SETTING: Airplane cabin. People are doing what people do in airplanes. A flight attendant limps up and down the aisle. A man politely stops her.

ATTENDANT (smiling with two front teeth missing)
Yes, sir, how can I help you?

MAN
Please get me a machine gun.

ATTENDANT
Surely.

Flight attendant exits and returns with a machine gun. She hands it to the man.

MAN (Jumping up and hastily penciling on a mustache)
Okay, nobody move, I'm hijacking this plane to Guam.

Everyone is terrified except for one man who has his eyes closed and headphones on. Another man leaps up and produces a grenade.

2nd MAN
Oh, no you're not. I'm hijacking this plane to Turkey.

1st MAN
Turkey? What the hell for?

2nd MAN
I like it there.

1st MAN
Wouldn't you rather go to Guam? Hmmm?

2nd MAN
Not reeeally…

Another man leaps up and takes a baseball bat out of his pants leg. The woman seated next to him looks disappointed.

3rd MAN
All right, I'm hijacking this plane to Sicily.

PILOT (sticking his head into the passenger compartment)
That's where we're going anyway.

3rd MAN
Forget it, then.

Another man jumps up, wielding a live snake.

4th MAN
Flight attendant, I'm hijacking this plane
to my grandmother's birthday party.

ATTENDANT
Surely.

1st MAN
Wait a second here! I got first dibs. We're going to Guam.

2nd MAN
Oh, man, Guam's nowheresville. Let's talk Turkey.

3rd MAN (forgetting what pilot has said)
Sicily!

4th MAN
Birthday!

The flight attendant begins passing out turtles as 3 of
the hijackers begin comparing travel brochures, with the
exception of the 4th hijacker, who produces Polaroids of his
grandmother's last birthday party. They argue over hotel
niceties, climate, and availability of fezzes. Finally, after
heated debate, the 1st hijacker faces the passengers, who
now all hold half-eaten turtles.

1st MAN
Okay, we've decided to go to Turkey. (Turns to hijacker 2)
And it better be good.

2nd MAN
Believe me, you'll never want to leave.

Suddenly, pilot enters cabin with a parachute on.

PILOT
I just won the lottery! I quit.

Pilot jumps from plane, at which the passengers notice that they have not been in a plane at all, but in a bus filled with helium (explaining everyone's silly voices). They slowly let the helium out, and drive into the city, where they eventually collide with an airplane that is taxiing down the street picking up bus passengers. An air traffic controller and bus passenger (both former hijackers) are blamed for the mix-up and are sent to prison for life, but only serve three months each because their grammar is horrible and they cannot finish their sentences (yeah, I know I used this line a couple stories ago).

ANGEL OF THE LORD

It was about 3 a.m. when an angel of the Lord appeared unto Bob (yes, unto Bob) in his bedroom.

Bob awoke with a start finish. The angel's wings fluttered mightily and sounded like heavy traffic (the latter was the only aspect of the angel that did not match the stereotype).

"Do not be afraid," said the angel in a soothing yet hollow voice.

The angel's words, however, were not heeded by Bob, who, upon seeing the half-human creature hovering over his bed, immediately went ape shit.

"Do not be afraid," repeated the angel.

Have you ever witnessed pure terror? Not the Hollywood type of terror, not the Janet Leigh in the shower in *Psycho* terror, but true, unadulterated, non-commercial terror? It's quite strange, actually. People revert to a primal state; they soil themselves; they adopt the mannerisms of a cornered animal. They shake their limbs and body haphazardly, as if they were on the Saturn equivalent of *Soul Train*. They do not scream, but emit mournful, deep bellows of bewilderment. Humanity and civility are erased.

And such was the terror of Bob, despite the angel's repeated message. In a bizarre twist of his torso, he threw himself from the bed and spasmodically made his way toward the door, as if he were on fire, as if a thousand wasps were stinging every square inch of his body. Bellowing gutturally, he threw himself through the door frame, took the stairs in one step, broke his neck during the tumbling descent, and slowly died, his eyes bulging, his mouth gasping. The angel disappeared.

The police, baffled by the lack of evidence, attributed Bob's suicide to a rare side effect of his antidepressant medication.

ONE KIND FAVOR

When I die, I want my corpse shot repeatedly out of a cannon into a brick wall, with a film of myself (shot beforehand) reacting comically at each impact. If this is too expensive, please seal every orifice of my corpse, fill me with helium, and release me.

Dream Loser

I dreamt last night that I was a might-has-been; a has-been that never was.

Famous Quotations from My Past Lives

"There is nothing to fear but big scary monsters."

"I have not yet begun to quit."

Proactivity

I read today that the average human being consumes 4 bushels of dirt over the course of a year. I ate my 4 bushels this morning to get it over with.

Human Speed Bumps

While driving, I saw a sign that read:

We have many children
But none to spare
So please, please
Drive with care

By the time I finished reading this ill-cadenced stanza, I had mowed down 5 toddlers.

Two Great Ideas By Me

Xerox paper to make more paper.

Make Love War not Hate War.

WRITER'S BLOCK

Author's Note: I had cancer. Making light of it is part of the treatment.

He applied a goodly amount of Writer's Block to his bod the day he visited Verbal Beach, but still got Editorial Skin Cancer cuz instead of re-applying Writer's Block every hour he re-applied to college every hour. He got that wrong.

They did The Biopsy. In the middle of The Biopsy, Butane, a first-year intern, noticed that the motions of all the team members during The Biopsy resembled an ensemble dance. He dubbed it "The Biopsy," and they toured to great acclaim. The difference between the Actual Biopsy and the Dance Biopsy was lost in the shuffle, and the janitors made the call: CANCER.

If only he had had ideas. If only he could say "I edited it" without tripping over his tongue. If only he hadn't been sexually attracted to only mice.

"But to the cancer, boys, we've got it, now let's deal with it."

This was his rallying cry as self-appointed leader of The

Cancer Boys, a group of unfortunates who met weekly at *TGI Fridays* to enjoy unlimited appetizers and try not to freak out.

"But you only have Editorial Skin Cancer," cried Lt. Col. Kipp "Bubble Dog" Schmalthington, a 17-year-old she-he-it-male with incurable cancer of the living room, "that's *nothing*."

"Nothing?!" cried Smellmania (the first revealing of our hero's name in this masterwork), "NOTHING?"

Smellmania disrobed to reveal the most disgusting array of welts, bruises, tattoos, piercings, and all-out cheese and hair that anyone with cancer had ever seen.

"Good Lord-o," yelped Svennsonn, who had cancer of the cancer, "I feel better now at having seen how Editorial Skin Cancer has ravaged his body, yah."

"And that ain't even the cancer," intoned Smellmania, "that's just my regular body. I was showing y'all the wrong side of me."

Smellmania twirled around, too effeminately for most, and revealed the ACTUAL damage done to his bod by ESC (I need to start abbreviating it now).

Upon looking at Smellmania's torrid backside, the entire room of cancer-riddled anti-lottery winners was cured, and instantly stood before him, normal and suddenly judgmental of those with cancer.

"EEEWWWW," they said in 17-part harmony. "It's like cottage cheese, it's like roadkill, it's like the plague, it's boiling over, it's festering, it's necrotized, it's not aesthetically pleasing whatsoever."

From that moment on, Smellmania (who had been a successful prognosticator until that moment) could only predict toast (and only after having seen bread put into a toaster).

He wandered the streets, alone unless he had friends who felt like wandering. He begged for scraps at the lumber yard, and thankfully wolfed down the bent nails and sawdust they tossed at his filthy garments. It was only when he changed into his laundered garments that they offered him a hamburger.

He looked pleadingly into the eyes of those emerging from limousines, hoping only to learn the correct spelling of "limousine." It was rock-bottom-time.

Like a dying diabetic who might as well enjoy ice cream, he strolled naked onto Larry Beach without applying Writer's Block. He did, however, apply Cinder Block, one to each shoulder fastened with bungee cords, and struggled to balance the concrete bricks while he purposely swaggered his newfound fine booty along the beach.

He worked hard for the money on his behind. (I should have written "he worked hard for the hiney.") Directly after the traumatic unveiling of his cancer-ridden doopah at The Cancer Boys meeting, upon which his buttocks were overwhelmingly reviled, he bought every workout video with the word "Buns" in it, and gauged his progress by checking out his hinterlands in anything reflective, including the sunglasses of strangers. It wasn't long before his ass was tasty.

The sun was unruly that day, and he found himself applying Cinder Block more often than not often compared with very often. Soon he looked like an outhouse in a cheap park, and despite his attempts to swagger-booty, he was now ensconced within a Cinder Block building and no one could see his behind.

But now what? Inside a Cinder Block building, ass wasted. He rigged a video screen to the outside wall of the structure he jogged within and simulcast the shift of his running buttocks.

It worked. The babes swarmed like way too many bugs. He was just about to get orgasm-face when the cancer thing came up again, and the babes got cold.

"Cancer? Pee-yew," they squealed, hopping into their soup-to-nuts StratoCaster and rocketing off to Pluto and The Moon. They were not there anymore.

Smellmania was at the end of his twine. It was the second-to-last cocktail straw. No, the last; we just checked.

He took a long, hard look at his life, and was instantly confused. Why was his life represented by various fish carcasses stacked on finely ground ice? He asked himself this question aloud, and a voice answered: "This ain't your life, buddy, it's the seafood department at Big Theodore's Food Universe."

It dawned on him like Tony Orlando. If he couldn't differentiate his life from a seafood department, he had bigger problems than cancer.

Bigger problems than cancer!

All the time he had been focusing on cancer, feeling sorry for his asshole, when he had bigger problems. Bigger problems than cancer. This startling new perspective on life so invigorated his mind, body, and soul that he laughed and cried at the same time, which looked stupid 'cause he so ugly.

"I've got bigger problems than cancer!" he shouted, riding horseback backwards incredibly slowly on the New Jersey Turnpike. Sadly, what he thought was newfound freedom turned out to suck very badly. "Cancer *and* other problems? Pee-yew to the max," said the world. He was even more ostracized, more shunned, more uninvited, more knocking at the door knowing full well that the lights were on and people were partying moments before.

"Sometimes solutions are problems," summarized

Smellmania, urinating into his own penis for whatever sustenance it could possibly provide. "But at least Jesus loves me."

"No I don't," said Jesus, ruining everything.

ONCE UPON A TIME THERE WAS A GOD

Once upon a time there was a God. He lived in Heaven with millions of angels that he created. He was perfect, he was incapable of creating anything bad, he was incapable of lying, and he was a God of love.

He then decided to create the world, all its heavenly bodies, oceans, land masses, plants, and animals. He then created man, and soon thereafter, woman. The Earth he created for the man and the woman to live upon was a paradise. There was no death, disease, sickness, sorrow, etc. So far so good.

One of the angels in heaven became jealous of God's power, and decided to tempt Adam and Eve (the man and woman) to eat from the fruit of the forbidden tree (God had put a forbidden tree into paradise, which held the key to good and evil...so to keep track of our crumbling perfection, we have jealousy, rebellion, evil, and a forbidden tree).

Satan, the rebellious angel (actually a misspelling of "Stan"), appeared to Eve in the form of a serpent, and tempted her, successfully, to break the rule about the forbidden tree. It was not odd to Eve that a snake was speaking to her. So, yeah.

Eve convinced Adam to also break the rule; Adam was obviously P-whipped, as Eve represented the only tang in Eden. Understandable.

Boy oh boy was the God of love mad. He threw Adam and Eve out of paradise, where they were left to grow old, contract diseases, and die. The God of love also hates injustice, so he decided that not only Adam and Eve but all of humanity would be sentenced to live with pain, suffering, and disease, like sentencing everyone in New Jersey to 5 years in prison for a robbery committed by one dude in Bayonne. As an added bonus, God threw Satan out of heaven and onto Earth, because it wasn't going to be hard enough down there already. (This was after a spirit war that occurred in heaven. Yep, a war in heaven.)

So, Satan rules the Earth and all of humanity suffers (well, most; some get lucky) because two idiots broke the first rule ever (no leniency based on first offense). The reason for this seeming master stroke of total injustice by the God that hates injustice is that God wants to prove to humans and Satan that people are better off under God's rule than under Satan's rule. This little game of "I told you so" is 3000 years old and going strong, although Biblical scholars tell us that we are living in the end times (as scholars in basically everyone's day advised).

But wait, there's more. At the end times, God will exhume everyone who ever lived (always wanted to meet Marilyn Monroe, didn't ya?), and Satan will be thrown into an abyss (couldn't God have done that in the first place?). Almost everyone who ever lived will be given the chance to adore God (some who God believes are hopeless will remain nonexistent, and some who have been extremely good will join the government of Heaven...yep, a government in Heaven), and the Earth will be rendered a paradise again like it was in the first place. The sharks will no longer use their 17 rows of razor-sharp teeth to eat humans and seals and other aquatic life. In paradise, the 17 rows of razor-sharp teeth will be used for...well, I don't have a clue, but, hey, we're back on track.

Everyone will fit on Earth, in case you're wondering, and all of Earth will resemble the prime real estate that we pay dearly for today, and not the scorched, barren plains of poverty and hopelessness that cover the present Earth because of naughty Adam and Eve.

After this blissful 1000 years, Satan will be released from the abyss for some reason and put back on Earth, proving that even the creator of history can't seem to learn from it, or that he really beats a dead horse when trying to make a point. Satan will once again try to persuade humans to follow his rule. Wow. Wonder what he'll use for bait. A bigger snake? This should be interesting.

Okay, here's the punch line: those that choose to follow Satan the second time around will be destroyed by the God of love because he hates injustice and is incapable of doing anything bad.

Lord, a little editing, if I may, and forgive me if I'm taking this all a bit too literally.

Cut out the whole middle part, even though it means that I'll probably have no record collection. We truly don't enjoy being the long-suffering pawns of your little spat with your ex-angel. So he challenged you. Get over it. This is your solution to that challenge? We deal with people challenging us all the time here on this Satan-ruled Earth, and we settle it without dragging billions of other people into the melee.

If you're a God of love, and you plan to one day show yourself, put us in paradise, and free us from all disease and suffering, we *will* enjoy it, trust me. We really didn't need this 3000 years of bullshit to arrive at the conclusion that we prefer paradise to, say, being kidnapped by a pedophile, tortured, chopped up, and put into a freezer. Yeah, I know, 3000 years is the blink of an eye to you...but, hey, it's not always about you.

The basic problem as I see it is that Adam and Eve had no perspective. All they knew was paradise. You created humans with the inability to identify light without darkness. If they had experienced even a day of disease and suffering, they would have left that tree alone. So here's an idea for your next planet: you're God, you can do anything, right?.... each person that you create will endure 1 day of Earthly horror (mental only; you can project the horror into their minds so that they don't actually get hurt, can't you?) and then be put in paradise, armed with the knowledge of what they'll have to live with if they fuck up.

Thanks for your time and attention. I truly hope that I meet you someday, and you explain all this more clearly than the knuckleheads presently telling me this story.

Amen.

I'M STORY

Every time I introduce my littlebrother Doge to someone, he burps through my armpits. My name is If. I am the eldest of three brothers, all the children of Mr. Sniw and his wife Garbedge.

When I was three I peed on my brother Salad and he told President Nixdude. I had to apologize televisionally in front of all channels. When I was seven, bears came out of my face, and my hair resembled a burning pigboff. They took me to the doctor, but he was crying. At this point my brother Salad had pushed himself off of sled and felt snowy. I remember when he traettled home that day, burst through the door and changed everybody, dick stuck in snowsuit zipper.

Yay, it's been hardlife. I went on and turned into a snarky man of twenty, too. My first job was washing boneheads at the goof wash. Unable to wash themselves because of stupid, the goofs would run criss crossy and snuckiling through ten rooms of suds. My job was to make sure. I was paid seventeen gibbons an hour, but only brought home three because of Government Smith.

I came home sweet home to the place I rented to find that

my gibbons had left ew in front of the TV (they had obviously been watching *The Lubboat* and *Barnaby Miller Jones and Wifebody*).

Get out here, I wrote to them weeks later. They skullied into the room, guilt ridden all over the facehole.

Before you say anything, began the widest gibbon, I must say Quuttons.

I was not hogboyed by his fooly.

Who left old ew by televiso? I almosted.

But it was not any of the gibbons! It was my long lostbrother Salad up into his olden trickens. Salad!

Suddenly everyone's grandparents surrounded me, dressed in their autobiographies, the most important chapters situated at eye level.

What do you want with me? I squirreled into tithery.

We want your tongue, they groaked, swirling toward me like tub drain working.

AAAHHH I said by instinct. They knocked me down by vote, and stepped on me until I thought I was a carpet. At that point, they convinced me that I was too big for the room, and that I had to be cut. When I saw them sliding off cacklying with my tongue, I knew I was not a carpet at all never.

My false tongue arrived in mailmanhands three days late, and I was happy but who could be happy? I put it in (the clips were a bitchee) and it looked so fake that I cried five. The only words I could say were "were" and "quaky," and quaky was already passé. If I wanted to say the words "Donald" and "eggboy" I would have to order another tongue, and so on. I mean, and soon.

I've gotten off trackle. I was telling youseses of my long and bump life. When I ten, I got my first meal for my birthday. It was a peanut and leaf with oil, and parent told me to suck on it and make it last, because my next meal would be my college gradation present.

College! Those were the yingy years! I was on team! I had an "A"! I roomed with Puke and Bottle, and the three of us funny. One time we partied at night and woke up feeling plop, but it was just like three musteers!

I changed my major from Why to Because in my sofa year. And when I was freshyman, I was noclue and pleshed a fratty! It wasn't long before nixdude. Those guys were silthy.

And old Perfezor Gg! Who could forget that old walty sirloin! Once he threw me outwards from class for chewying gump. I said, This ain't isn't Hi skoo, and got voted class clown jones. Then my pants fell down in the middle of class and I got voted most blendy.

Then luhf. It was the first day in Introduction to Groupbody, and she sat down right in front of Brolly, which is me nicknamewise. Her hair smelled like piny place and I wanted to reach out and touch it, but my arms are two inches long. Mad with unreturnable luhf, I bit her head in three. She responded with oxgaggle, and consented to be wifehead. We were married and divorced in one day because she found out that I had Kwinty of the Intesto.

Brokharted, I returned home to find I had only been gone three minutes. My brother Salad had pooped in tub, and Granpy was running to the barn to bury his legs. It was goody to be home, but my stemp farther Blillee was still beatying my mother. I called policy, and they arrested my brother Salad for pooping tub. Which leads me to how I helped Salad break out of prissy. I carved a cell out of soap and sent it to Salad in a cakey. Salad washed himself so clean with the soap that he slid out through the cell bars. He stole the guard's keys and locked himself back in his cell, remembering that he had cakey left. By that time I had a gorilla (who went by the name "Go-Rilly" to avoid detection) hooked up to the cell window, and it pulled the whole side of the prison off. Everyone escaped, and the President granted everyone a pardon because he burped.

With a degree in bachelorism in my hand and a new attitude under my belt, I threw myself into workworld and squoze into my nicky in sosighety. I got a job as a traveling machine imitator, and saved enough gibbons to start a small hot dog roll stand. A hot dog vendor opened across the street from me, and business was boom. One of the gibbons suggested that we add on a resterroom and I peed on him. I decided to add mustard to my inventory, and when a ketchup stand opened next door, we merged all the businesses, pooled our gibbons, and wore chaps. At one of the business meetings Duffyoe said, Why don't we get napkies that say "Have Nicie," and we bought out his third of the business and lizardized him. Now he is working as the city punching bag.

Now it was just me and McFace. I didn't trust him because he had eyebrows where his sideburns should have been, and armpit hair where his eyebrows should have been, and his legs came out of his armpits, and his sideburns were where his legs should have been...besides that he lied constantly. One day I came into work and he was on the floor with Bitch, the local fucky girl. He was drunk laffy!

Has anyone prepared today's dogs for the 9:07 rush? I quested. Bitch giggled and rolled over, her bellie big as all outdoor. McFace had fed her all our hot dogs to entice her toward penis! That's quite enough it, I yelled...

Wake up, Dorfy from only dream!

And it was, although what a copout. I was lying in my bed at camp Sassy, looking up at half my friends.

But, but you, Stankbamb, were the man who was scared of crows! And Frelly, you were the lion and cow ward! And Blemish, you were the man with the hot tin cat roof! And Gobbleplaque! You were the Wizoz of Ard!

Then out of left outfield comes Sportsball Hallway Flamer Ruth Babey. "There's no plate like home," sez The Babey, signing our balls.

MILLIONS

Their million-dollar ideas spilled from their mouths like a thousand bucks and hit the ground like wooden nickels.

"Got one," said Useless, half drunk only because he couldn't count, "The Hang-a-Mooners. You find actors that look just like Gleason, Carney, Meadows, and Randolph, you have them re-enact the same scripts, word for word, but whenever they enter the room, they hang a big moon. Like, for example, when Ralph comes in the door at the beginning of the episode from work, and that little bit of intro music is playing and the audience is applauding, he'll put his hat down on that dresser, put down his lunch box, then drop his pants and hang a big moon while calling "Alice, I'm home!" Then Alice would come in amidst more applause, immediately hike up her dress, pull down the back of her panties, chuck a moon at Ralph, and go into whatever dialog she has. Same thing for Norton; he bursts in the door, and makes all these gestures like he's going to hang a moon but doesn't, and then Ralph gets impatient and yells 'Will you come on!!!' and then Norton finally hangs a moon."

"And I guess the show's intro would be that moon rising to reveal a picture of Ralph's ass instead of his face, and then the rising asses of the successive cast members instead of the extra rising moons, right?" asked Beltway.

"That's brilliant!" said Useless. "I never thought of that!"

"That's the *first* thing you should have thought of," said Beltway. "I mean, that's when the announcer would say 'Jackie Gleason...The Hang-a-Mooners...with the stars Art Carney' etcetera."

"Million dollar ideas, just falling out of our brains, destined for decay. We'll never do anything with these ideas. We're gifted but not driven. We're idea men; we need action men to take these ideas and put them into, well, action," lamented Useless.

"Maybe we don't want to be millionaires because if we have everything we ever wanted and are still unhappy, there will be absolutely nowhere else to turn and that would be devastating. You know, like Cobain," mused Beltway.

"Nirvana was excellent!" yelled Useless, opening his last beer before his heart attack.

ROUTINE

I am a creature of routine. I wash each body part in the same order during my morning shower, and dry myself in the exact same manner afterward. When powering down my automobile upon arriving from work, my actions are always the same: radio off, ignition off, keys in hand, heater/air conditioner (dependent upon the season) off, open door, flip door lock, exit car, shut door, lock door.

If anything out of the ordinary occurs during the aspects of my life I have devoted to routine, I become confused, and something goes awry. If my wife asks me to find her sunglasses before I exit the house, I will forget my lunch. If there is a sudden appearance of my daughter in the bathroom while I am showering, and she asks whether Bugs Bunny has been in the room, I will forget whether I've shampooed.

Today was a prime example of a chink in my routine that led to an embarrassing snafu: I inadvertently locked my keys in my car due to the distraction caused to my routine by a carjacker.

It started out innocently enough. I was cruising down local

route 542 East when I saw him standing by the edge of the road, waving his arms in distress. I should have known something was wrong when I stopped, he got in, I continued driving, I asked him for a cigarette, he produced one, and lit it for me...all the time still waving his arms in distress.

"You can stop waving your arms in distress," I said. "Where do you need to go?"

He abruptly stopped waving his arms, looking at them both in embarrassment as if they were stupid accomplices.

"I'm sorry," he said. "I waved my arms much too long, but you see, I'm not very good at this yet."

"Good at what?" I asked.

"Carjacking," he said.

"Carjacking?" I repeated. "I should say you're not very good. You're supposed to drag me from the car, slap me down, and take off in my vehicle. I think what you're doing is simply hitchhiking."

"No," he said. "You stick out your thumb when you hitchhike. I was waving my arms in distress."

"Yes, I remember," I said. "Well, you're neither hitchhiking or carjacking. You're just riding under a false pretense."

"Can't one carjack by holding a gun to the driver's head and making him drive one somewhere?" he queried.

"Hmmm, maybe...but I'm not sure if that's not kidnapping. Besides, why would you want anybody else to drive? I don't know. Maybe that could qualify as carjacking, if you had a gun and couldn't actually drive because of a broken wrist or something."

The would-be carjacker pulled a gun from his jacket, pointed it at my head, and broke his wrist with a scream of anguish.

"NOW am I carjacking, wise ass?" he shouted.

"Yes," I answered.

Now, I'm not one to bow to the politically correct mores of society, and I would have no trouble whatsoever identifying the race, gender, and national origin of my assailant, but truth be told he was an exact replica of myself save the fact that he had only one nostril.

"What are you staring at? Keep your eyes on the road," my assailant yelled.

"I'm staring at you...or, me...you look exactly like me, except for the nostril."

"Well, you're pretty smart for an asshole," he said. "Part two of my carjacking crime is I'm gonna steal your identity."

"By looking like me?"

"No, moron...I mean, yes, moron, but that's the final step. I've been following you for years...making bogus charges on your credit cards...committing crimes in your name all over the country." He ran down a list of the things he had purchased and the crimes he had committed.

"Well, it's no wonder I never noticed," I said. "I bought the exact same stuff and committed the exact same crimes."

"Well, now I'm you, and I've had the plastic surgery to make us identical. I'm taking over your whole life, buddy."

"But the nostril..."

"Hey, you think any plastic surgeon in the universe is going to be able to replicate that steam shovel above your lips without screwing up a little? Cut me a fucking break."

That hurt. All my life I had been called Big Nose, to the point where I had heard the term so much and so often that I actually wore it like a badge of honor. I began calling myself Big Nose, calling others with big noses Big Nose, and letting them call me Big Nose back, creating a Big Nose brotherhood where we could all find solace...and we never let anybody with small noses call us Big Nose. No; they had to gingerly debate and discuss the fact that they were not allowed to use the "BN" word.

I pulled in to work, began to power down my automobile, and, due to the distraction to my routine caused by the carjacker, locked my keys (and the carjacker) in my car.

I shouted to the carjacker through the closed window "Open the door."

"No," he said.

"But I've locked my keys in the car," I explained.

"No shit, asshole, but I ain't helpin' ya."

A moment passed.

"Well, what are you going to do?" I shouted. "Why don't you just drive away? You've got the keys and the car."

"I can't drive a stick," he said sadly.

"Then give me the goddamn keys and I'll teach you," I lied.

"Oh, no you don't. I ain't fallin' for that one again," he said angrily, holding the gun to the window.

"Well, screw this," I said. "I'm going in to work. I'm late as it is."

"You mean *I'm* late," he yelled, "or have you forgotten that I'm stealing your identity?"

His face betrayed that he'd suddenly had an idea, and before I could react, he jumped out of the car, keys in hand, and locked it behind him. We eyed each other for a split second, and then both began running toward the entrance to the building in which I worked.

We got to the door at the same time, and I could have killed myself after courteously opening the door for him; stupid! He was in my office three steps ahead of me, and sat down in front of my computer.

"How do you turn this thing on?" he demanded.

"Oh, c'mon!" I said "I thought you'd been watching me for years!"

"*Not all the time*," he whined, "and mostly at your house."

My boss, Rock and Roll Ronald, entered the office, looked at the both of me, and corporated "OK, so you cloned yourself because of the heavy workload but I'm still only paying you guys one salary."

My identity theft/carjacker, having dropped his toothpaste, was crestfallen. "How am I ever going to get ahead?" he lamented. He scribbled a suicide note that simply read "Bread, milk, eggs, TP, cat food" and shot himself. Because of his meticulous preparation regarding his theft of my identity, we both died, but not before I quickly scribbled "orange juice" onto the list.

INFECTION

I remember the first time I saw her, on Rock n' Roll Bob's T-shirt, getting spanked, and the indescribable feeling I had...infection, obsession, love, lust, desperation, longing, astonishment, awe, helplessness, a sense of being stunned. There was no word for it.

"Who's that?" I asked, attempting calm, although my voice cracked and the ringing in my ears made the question sound as if it came from somewhere other than my own head.

Rock n' Roll Bob looked down absently at his T-shirt, as if someone else had dressed him and he had no idea what he was wearing (which was probably the case).

"Bettie Page," he murmured, his voice dripping with stupid cool. "ID."

Even though Rock n' Roll Bob knew exactly who and how old I was, the club had been raided for underage drinking recently and everyone had to show ID, even the old men who used to drink at the club in the 40s when it was a respectable joint and still sat like ghosts at the bar staring into the same drinks while the world changed around them like time-lapse photography.

I didn't register Rock n' Roll Bob's request for identification. "Yeah, but who *is* she?" My mouth was marijuana dry; my heart beat so urgently it qualified as exercise.

"Pin-up icon," he mumbled, then a shade louder, "ID."

I became aware of the line of leather-clad, glue-hairdo'd clientele forming behind me, and fumbled for my wallet as I stared a hole through Rock n' Roll Bob's T-shirt.

"Where'd you get the shirt?"

"Don't know."

I stepped inside the bar, grabbed a stool within eyeshot of the shirt, and continued staring. Rock n' Roll Bob was used to being stared at, but he grew increasingly uncomfortable, so I left my beer half finished and jettisoned myself out the back door of the club and onto the street, a blind headlong rush home to my computer and the Internet, repeating the name over and over to myself until it caused stricture in my chest and spasms in my crotch.

———— ((●)) ————

It was empty pool swan dive when the Internet slapped me with the truth: Bettie Page was my age in 1952. And, oh, how many hits, how many sites, how many fans, how many worshippers…and how did I come to live my entire life up to this point unaware of her?

Each picture I *clicked to enlarge* made me increasingly dizzy. My blood churned like floodwaters; my printer nearly caught fire. I stayed up all night, her pictures spread all over my bed. When I found out (that same night) that Bettie Page was still alive, I vowed to myself that I would meet her. In the meantime, and much like the haste with which Noah must have built the ark, if that story is even true, I consumed and collected all things Bettie Page until my apartment was a shrine, my mind was a memory bank of her life, and my friends were very worried. I had books, original magazines, original photographs, reproduced photographs, films, authorized biographies, unauthorized biographies, life-sized cardboard cutouts (which I went through very quickly, and please do not judge me, but try to understand my indescribable feelings for her), buttons, badges, pins, watches, magnets, portraits, audiotaped interviews…the only thing I didn't have was Bettie herself, but I had a plan.

Again, you must try and understand. Please put yourself in my place, even though I know in my soul that it's not possible… have you ever had a feeling that you couldn't describe, and can attribute that feeling to a single person, a person who does not share your same age-time and age-space, a person who you've never even met but know intimately? Can you comprehend that making love to this angel, despite the difference in ages, is something that I absolutely *had* to do, because she is actually still sharing the planet with me, that she is *still here*? That such lovemaking has nothing at all to do with base desires, but to a communion that, much like my feelings for her, transcends the common lexicon of explanation, definition, and understanding? A *timeless* communion, *time travel* in and of itself via two commingling souls...can you possibly understand that?

Bettie Page is a recluse, living in California, and has refused to be seen or photographed by the public since the late 1950s, when she dropped out of sight (two rare exceptions exist courtesy of the power of *Playboy* magazine). That much I knew. But I also knew that, unlike her other "fans," I was seeking a communion with her (I shall use this term henceforth), a communion that she, as a lady of God (she became a born-again Christian after her pin-up days) would certainly recognize and understand.

Did I mention that the Internet is a beautiful thing, an organized, global library dumped in your lap without dusty Dewey Decimal Systems, card catalogs, or shushing old maids? If there is one thing I can say for my plight, it is that I am glad it did not occur in the 1970s...what I learned about Bettie in one night in February 2006 would have taken me a decade of intense research in the era before the Internet. On one inspired evening, and in approximately 10 clicks, I had located the individual who wrote, with the help of Bettie herself, the authorized Bettie Page biography. I gathered every dime I could amass, that is, every dime of credit I was qualified for, $20,000 worth, and got aboard a plane to

California to pay a surprise visit to Bettie's biographer and offer him $20,000 for her address.

—)(◍)(—

Can I tell you how easy a transaction it was? Can I tell you that money talks, that everything is for sale, and that cash trumps loyalty? A knock at the door...a "yes, can I help you?" A question to confirm the identity of the biographer, and then a simple statement: "It is imperative that I commune with Bettie Page, and I'm prepared to offer you $20,000 simply for her address." Will I step inside? Will I promise to never reveal how I got the address? Will I ensure that promise by producing my identification and providing *my* address, should, God forbid, anything go awry? Can I show him the money, in this case a cashier's check?

A search for a pen and a piece of paper; a scribble; the simultaneous address/check hand-off, and I was back outside, sweating like a triathlete and shaking like a rattlesnake.

Bettie was 3 hours away, and I won't say where, not that it matters now. I drove my rented Acura directly to her address (thank you again modern technology for your on-board navigational systems) and knocked on the door, fate at my side, out of my own body and peering down from above, my head helium, legs concrete, heart full of dynamite.

When she answered, I fainted face-first into a large potted plant.

———((O))———

I came to on her couch, a cold compress on my forehead, a cup of tea waiting. She hovered above me like an angel, and she was, and when I blinked myself back into consciousness, feeling as if it were all a dream beginning with Rock n' Roll Bob's T-shirt, she smiled down at me, her hand on mine, and asked in her famous Southern drawl how I would like my tea. My body surged with millions of volts; I was sure sparks were flying from my every cavity.

"I love you," was all I could manage to say, and it sounded as if I were ready to cry.

She took the compress from my forehead, folded it, put it aside on an end table. "I know," she said, and I lay stunned as she removed her blouse and let it fall to the floor. I audibly groaned. Her bra fell away next, and she stood to remove her pants, and then her panties. Was I groaning? Was I moaning? Was I crying? Yes, yes, and yes...she still had her trademark black bangs, and I saw the flicker of precocious youth clinging to her eyes...yes, time had trampled on, and she was no longer the vision she once was, far from it, but you must remember that ours was to be a timeless communion, and that time travel would be invented the moment we embraced, and it was.

Is there a state beyond out-of-body? Is there an experience above uber-nirvana? I was not only hovering above myself as Bettie hovered over me, I was hovering over the heavens, over the entire infinite (or finite, should they figure it out) universe; I was my own God, watching with great rapture as the only two people on Earth consummated their timeless communion.

I felt thereafter like a being composed of pure glowing energy. I sat in a state of electric calm, sipping tea as we talked about her life: about her sexually abusive father, the scholarship she didn't get that broke her heart, the momentous day she changed her hairstyle on the advice of a photographer she met by happenstance, about her broken dreams of being an actress, her underground groundbreaking work for the Klaws, the Senate hearings, her disappearance, her religious conversion, her anonymous retroactive reemergence. During a pause in the conversation I moved toward her in a trance and kissed her from the top of her head to the soles of her feet before communing once again.

⸻ ◉ ⸻

The glaring sunlight that had been clawing at the drawn blinds slowly gave up its attempt to illuminate the room, and she looked at me suddenly, ethereally, as if out of a dream, and said "You must go now." I'd lost track of time, and couldn't tell whether I'd been lying next to her after our second communion for 2 minutes, 2 hours, or 2 days. I looked into her face, my tears flowing freely, and answered "I know." It was as if I was carrying my own body toward the door, my carcass a ton but my soul light as ether. At the door, I gave her a parting kiss.

"You mustn't return," she said. "Please remember our time together. Please remember me when you look at my photos from my modeling days. Please remember me how I was."

"I will remember you as you were, and as you are, the most captivatingly beautiful soul on this Earth," I answered, and she did me the ultimate favor and kindness of not retreating inside and closing the door until I had driven out of sight, because, frankly, I could not have lived through the sound.

<hr/>

A stack of mail awaited me when finally I returned to my apartment-turned-Bettie-Page-shrine. I flipped through the bills and junk mail like an electronic sorter, gazing up at the pictures of my sweet Bettie in between letters. I had seen myself sitting atop every cloud that passed my window on the plane trip home, and I wondered now, as I performed a function so banal as reviewing my mail, whether my feet would ever meet terra firma again. I was exploding and calm, melancholy and joyful, thrilled to be alive and ready to die. There was no higher point to which I could rise; I could only hope to maintain my heavenly station through memory.

The mail also included an overnight delivery, from California, and I tore open the cardboard to find a personal letter within an envelope...my heart began beating wildly, and tears began to flow as if weeping were suddenly an autonomic function. I carefully opened the letter, preparing myself for the sweet blissful escape Bettie's words—her thoughts regarding our communion—would provide; before even throwing my teary gaze upon the letter, I had already made plans to read it over and over through the night, her pictures spread all around me. My hands trembled as I pulled the paper from within the envelope, and as I did, a cashier's check—my cashier's check—for $20,000 fell from within and onto the ground. I was stunned, confused by the sight of it, and unfolded the letter:

Dear Mr. Pierce:

Enclosed please find your cashier's check in the amount of $20,000 that I accepted in exchange for Bettie Page's address last Tuesday, March 14. I must apologize for the slight deception, but you would be shocked (or perhaps you wouldn't) by the number of people who contact me on a weekly basis in search of Bettie Page, some offering as much as $200,000 simply for her address. Bettie herself suggested the *notion of sponsoring a "look-alike" at the address you visited, so that her fans could enjoy a "virtual" meeting with Bettie Page, or at least the next best thing. We took great care in selecting Amanda, who Bettie herself trained in the art of conversation about her life and times. Bettie and I hope that you weren't too disappointed when Amanda told you of her true identity, and that your check would be returned. We hope that your conversation with her was satisfying. We have spoken with Amanda and she told us you were a perfect gentleman (some fans have actually tried to assault Amanda; we therefore station bodyguards outside the house). Thank you so much for supporting, remembering, and being a fan of Bettie Page.*

I wasn't aware that my knees had buckled, and I hit the ground hard, the letter floating after me and landing on my chest. I hadn't been able to read very far past the phrase "look-alike" due to the indescribable feeling that came over me—astonishment, numbness, helplessness, desperation, mortification, tragedy, infection...there was no word for it.

BANG BANG

I leapt from the couch and pounded both my fists upon the anger table (I had never had coffee on this table, but pounded it nightly with my fists in rage while watching the evening news). "That's it," I that's-itted, "I'm getting a goddamn gun!"

The evening news that evening had run a story about the fact that I was the only person in America who didn't have a gun.

"I want a gun," I said, entering the police station. A police officer approached me, and I couldn't help but notice that the brass name plate on his chest read "Offisser."

"So you want to exercise your right to bear arms?" he asked.

"That's right," I said.

He leapt over the counter that divided us, grabbed my shirt at the shoulders, and violently ripped my sleeves off.

"There," he said dryly. "Bare arms."

All the policemen in the room were cracking up doughnuts.

"That's an evergreen," said officer Offisser. I looked down conspicuously at his name plate, and he took notice.

"Yeah, yeah, yeah," he said, "go ahead. I heard it all."

"So your name is actually officer Offisser," I asked/said. His colleagues began to chuckle doughnut holes.

"Maybe you'd just better change yer goddamn name," said another cop, filing blank papers.

"You change *your* goddamn name," said officer Offisser. The other officer turned, pissed, and his name plate became visible: "Kopp."

"Why should I change my name, huh?" he mirror-sunglassed. The commotion caused a higher-ranking cop to burst into the room.

"That's enough out of both of you!" the high-ranking cop shouted. "I wish you'd both change your names so we wouldn't have to go through this crap every two and a quarter seconds!"

"You're right, Sergeant Rolman," they both said in sheepish unison.

"Your first name's 'Pat,' right?" I said to Sergeant Rolman.

"Oh my God, how'd you know???" said Rolman, amazed. The other cops borrowed some of Rolman's amazement and looked at me with it.

"My gun?" I reminded.

"Here," said Offisser, tossing me his gun. "Just don't hurt anybody."

I turned to exit.

"Hey," Rolman began, "did I notice correctly that you do NOT have a PBA sticker on the windshield of your vehicle?"

"That's right, I don't, but..."

"Well, here's a ticket for that violation," he said.

"Why am I getting a ticket for not having a PBA sticker in my window?" I asked, incredulous. I thought of pulling my new gun and killing them all, but didn't have any bullets yet.

"Well," began Rolman, "a lot of folks believe that if they *have* a PBA sticker in their window, it will get them out of tickets, so we decided to do the opposite and give people tickets who *don't* have PBA stickers...make sense?"

———⊶((◉))⊷———

I arrived home with my new gun to find a burglar in my house pointing a gun to my wife's head. My wife was on her knees on the floor, fast asleep due to a recent addiction to sleep medication (the manufacturer of the sleep medication claimed that their product was non-addictive unless you started to depend on it).

I pulled my bullet-less gun and said "drop the gun."

"You drop the gun," the burglar retorted.

"I asked you first," I said.

"Well, I hardly think this situation falls under the umbrella of standard etiquette," said the burglar. "Drop the gun or your wife gets it...I mean, I assume she's your wife."

"Yes, that's my wife," I confirmed. "If you've been through the house, you'll know from the pictures on the walls that it's my wife."

My wife snored, awakening momentarily to mutter something about milk and cookies before falling back asleep.

"Milk and cookies," echoed the burglar, "that was so cute."

"Yeah," I said, "she likes milk. And cookies. Well, the two together, really. Milk *and* cookies. Combined..."

Mindless, rambling conversation? Yes...but quite intentional, for as I blathered on, I attached the fake dangling arms to my shoulders that I bought at the gun shop for just this type of predicament...with the fake arms attached, I loaded my gun behind my back.

"Aha!" I shouted, drawing my weapon (I wanted to achieve Eastwood in that moment, but only got Kramden bursting in on Alice when he thought she was cheating). The burglar was momentarily confused by my four arms, and then, figuring it out, yelled "fake dangling arms for covert behind-the-back gun-loading! God damn you!"

Gunfire ensued. The burglar and I took several shots at each other, none successful. We paused, realizing we both sucked.

"I just got this gun," I explained.

"First day as a burglar," he admitted. "Maybe we should get closer together."

I considered his suggestion for a millisecond.

"Closer together my ass," I spat, "what the hell are you doing in my house anyway?"

"Just doing my job, man," he said defensively.

"Job?" I echoed, gasted by the flabber.

"Yeah, man, due to the extraterrestrials taking all the jobs that the illegal aliens won't do, the Department of Labor classified burglary as a profession in order to reduce unemployment."

That explained all the burglary courses I'd seen in the local community college fliers.

"Listen, I didn't even get your name," I said, suddenly remembering my manners.

"Can I give you an alias?" the burglar responded, "After all, I am a burglar."

I nodded my head.

"John Doe."

"John Doe?" I mocked. "Real creative."

"Well, excuse me," said alleged Doe, annoyed, "but I'm not going to expend my creative energy on an alias when it's better served trying to figure out how I'm going to extricate myself from this situation, hopefully with all of your riches and without killing anybody...Geez, they go over this stuff in burglary class, but experience is really the only teacher, y'know?"

Doe and I both looked, astonished, to the figure who had just burst through the door. Officer Offisser!

Offisser took out an extremely small notepad and addressed us both.

"Did anyone say 'drop the gun?' And if so, who said it first?" asked Offisser.

"Who cares?" lamented Doe, "I'm just trying to feed my family."

"We ran a background check on you," said Offisser, "you have no family."

"I *am* my family," protested Doe. "It's legal in Boston as of yesterday to marry yourself and declare yourself to be your own children."

It was then that Offisser closed his notebook and declared that I was at fault for amassing riches and tempting burglars to steal them.

Now, I'm not one to be afraid of political correctness and shy away from revealing the gender, race, and national origin of my assailant, but truth be told, he looked exactly like me, a carbon copy, the only difference being that I was a gifted singer and he was only capable of back-up vocals, maybe the occasional feature song.

Officer Offisser suddenly noticed our physical similarity. "What are you guys, twins?" he said, his moustache growing before our eyes.

"Not exactly," I said. "He can't sing, I can."

"Your broad ass I can't," said Doe.

"Let's settle this," commanded Offisser. "What tune?"

"Everyday I Have the Blues," my unconscious wife perisomnambicly suggested.

"What version though?" said Offisser. "You got the original Lowell Fulson version, the Joe Williams version..."

"There were actually two recordings by Williams," Doe interjected, "one with the Count Basie Orchestra and one geared to the R&B market on Checker, a subsidiary of the famous Chess label."

"...and the BB King version," Offisser finished.

We settled on the Joe Williams version with the Basie Orchestra (Offisser singing the horn parts), and, inevitably, Doe was found to be lacking.

"Whatever," said Doe after the announcement was made by Offisser. Doe was pissed, dejected. It was always like this, he thought. Always second best; no one recognized his greatness. He heard himself in his ears. He was a star. Unstoppable. What the fuck did they know? Suddenly he got pissed at everything, even my writing.

"What kind of shit is this, anyway?" spat Doe, reading my work due to his sudden ability to render himself sentient thanks to super-highly-advanced technology provided by aliens during a recent and benevolent visit (these same aliens also wrote all of The Beatles' songs).

"Farts, I think," Offisser answered, he too becoming sentient.

"You mean *farce*, right?" said Doe.

"Yeah, yeah, *farce*, whatever," Offisser spittled. "Some ancient literary form no one cares about."

"Well, it exists, marginally," I said to my recent fellow humans, "but you can't call it 'farce' because it will turn people off. You have to call it something more broad and accessible, like 'comedy.' *Spinal Tap* is an example. *Pulp Fiction*, also farcical, was more successful than *Tap*, at least initially, but that's probably because Tarantino was smart enough to pander to his audience and render his brilliant dialog awash with blood."

"Well, you can't call *this* comedy, can you? I mean, it's not particularly funny," judged Doe.

"But what's funny these days?...I mean, shock value has rendered the public as impatient with comedy as they are with microwave meals (Doe made himself a mental note to write himself a note on a piece of paper about putting microwaves into faster microwaves to speed cooking). Everything has to be instantaneous...we've actually come full circle and are back in the days of slapstick, except that everything's sex, sex, sex...so instead of a pie hitting you in the face, it's..." I reached...

"Genitals?" offered Offisser...

"Yeah, genitals hitting you in the face," I concluded.

"That *is* pretty funny if you think about it...y'know, genitals unattached from the body, thrown from a distance at a good clip and making noise when they hit your face...and then plopping to the floor with some sort of 'thud' or 'squirt,' depending on the gender. And of course, the subsequent facial expression of the person who gets hit," Doe mused.

"Yeah...like the classic double-take of James Finlayson or the trademark slow burn of Edgar Kennedy...well, maybe some parts of this crap *are* funny, I guess, but not to everybody... what does the author even call this stuff? Can you check the cover or inner book flap to see if he defines it?" queried Offisser.

"Book flap? Are you kidding? Oh, cue the god damn laugh track...this ain't no book. This is 'waste-of-computer,' or 'vanity publishing'...and if it's the latter, he probably can't afford hard cover with a book flap," Doe court-jestered.

"Wait...*Yessov Korsukan*, a Russian immigrant from another 'story' of his, told me that he refers to his writing as 'literary doodles' or some such nonsense, probably because he can't focus long enough to write a proper short story...he's desperate to entice someone to read this drivel, as if he has something to say," offered Offisser.

"And the saddest part of it is that he's banging away at his keyboard as we speak, desperately trying to keep up with our dialog because of the super-highly-advanced technology that allows us to render ourselves sentient beyond our non-existent computer-text-generated selves, thus able to read/create the text before us. He's too stupid to figure out that if he wants us to stop denigrating his work, all he has to do is stop typ

ABOUT THE AUTHOR

Picture Me!

Jim Wood arrived in America in 1376, and was told to come back after the country had been "discovered," wrested from its native inhabitants, colonized, and rendered independent. Wood followed that advice and was born to a middle class couple in 1963 in central New Jersey. He led a happy and relatively uneventful childhood, which led to a more turbulent, angst-filled adolescence, which finally blossomed into an angry, confused, and bewildered adulthood masked by unending mirth. He currently lives with his wife and daughter in a house built in 1850 (474 years after his initial arrival in what would become America). He owns approximately 5000 78 and 45 rpm rhythm and blues records from the golden era of roots rock (1946-1954), and likes beer a whole lot, maybe too much.